The Motherless Children

By

CaSaundra W. Foreman-Harris

1stBooks - rev. 12/11/01

ACKNOWLEDGEMENTS

A blessing—that's what it is…a blessing from God to be able to write, and publish another book.

I would like to take this time to thank each of you who supported me with my first book, *When An Angel Takes Flight*. Thanks for your kind words and for your encouragement, by letting me know that you were anxious to read my next project.

To my mother, Lorene Foreman, I say thanks again for backing me and encouraging me to continue to use the talents that God blessed me with. I love you.

To my oldest son, Marquis, I'm proud of the young man you are becoming. Remember that God will never put more on you than you can bear. I love you.

To my youngest son, LaBraska; Remember God's eye is always on the sparrow. He's watching over you. I love you.

To my husband, Sheldon; thanks for your support. Remember, what's to come is better than what's been. I love you.

To my friend LaSonia Stewart, thanks for your help, support and prayers.

To all of my friends, true friends, thanks for having my back and for positive thoughts and prayers. May God Bless You.

And last, but most importantly, to God, thank you for blessing me with talent, faith, patience and belief in myself. With you, I know that all things are possible.

In Memory and
Celebration of the lives of:

Laura Brown

Jessie Halstied

Daisy Harris

&

Dayle Faye Cotton-Walker

I'm thankful for the opportunity God
blessed me with by allowing these
women to be a part of my life. I know
they're safe in His arms…

This book is dedicated to mothers and daughters everywhere, whose inner beauty, exceeds their outer beauty, and allows them to appreciate the image they see in the mirror —CWFH ☆

TABLE OF CONTENTS

CHAPTERS

x

Dear Reader:

I've always found the relationship between mothers and daughters an interesting subject. Because my relationship with my own mother has been filled with it's high points and it's low points, and we still share a bond that will never be broken, I find it fascinating to hear mother's talk about their relationship with their daughters and hear daughters discuss their relationship with their mothers.

When I think about my mother, I think about the woman who taught me right from wrong. I think about the woman who bathed me, clothed me, fed me, read to me, rocked me to sleep, bandaged my scraped knees, and gave me an ice cold bath once because she couldn't get my fever down. I think about the woman who disciplined me, taught me responsibility, instilled values in me, hugged me, encouraged me to do my best at all times, pushed me to do "better than", and to use my brain for more than just to part my ears. I think about the woman who proved that she loved me. Now, I'm a mother, and I'm trying to learn how to be a good parent. And, my mother still teaches me, just as she did when I was her little girl.

Mother's in general teach us about responsibility and about life. They teach us about our bodies, about sex, and about the opposite sex. They teach us about independence and self-discipline. They encourage cleanliness, and lady-like mannerisms. They demand self-respect and pride from us.

As a daughter, there were so many demands placed on me by my mother that I often didn't understand why she was so mean to me. Why did I have to wash dishes, and fold clothes, and make the bed, and keep my room clean? Why did I have to clean the bathroom and take out the trash and iron my clothes and dust the furniture? Why did I have to say please and thank you and yes ma'am, and no ma'am? Why did I have to remember to sit with my legs closed when I wore a dress, and why did I have to sit up straight? Why couldn't I wear make-up in the seventh grade? Why couldn't I have a boyfriend until I was seventeen? And why is it that every time I would say to my mother, "but everybody else is..." my mother, (the woman who is so sweet, and kind, and concerned) didn't care what "everybody else is..." because until they start to clothe you and feed you, she just really doesn't care to discuss it any further? Why couldn't I wear my favorite white shoes in the winter, and printed panties under my light colored pants? Why couldn't I talk to strangers, and why couldn't I ride in a car with a boy I didn't know? Why couldn't I take money from boys if they wanted to give it to me? Why did she look at me like she'd forgotten I was her baby, and was about to strangle me, just because I told a half-truth?

Why? Why is more than just because she said so. Why? I know why now. Because she knew what I didn't know. She knew that someday, I was going to grow up, and if she wasn't "mean" to me, I wouldn't make it. She taught me what was necessary to make it in this world. Now, whether or not I digested all the knowledge my mother tried to feed me is another story.

Mothers teach their daughters the same things their mothers taught them. If we pay attention, we can learn an important element to life: wisdom.

Now, imagine your mother never taught you anything. Imagine...she didn't care enough about you to see you grow up. Imagine she never told you she loved you. Imagine she abandoned you. Imagine she left a scar so deep in your heart, that you couldn't feel anything for anyone, not even your own children.

Hard to imagine isn't it? But the image you see…is real. Somewhere out there, mothers are actually doing these things to their children, to their daughters, leaving these innocent children, motherless.

This book, The Motherless Children, is the story of children abandoned by their mother, and the affects her abandonment has on them.

It is my prayer that you will allow yourself some free time to relax and open your heart, while you walk through this emotional, yet exhilarating journey.

There is a poem in this story called *What Matters*. Credit for this poem in the story is given to Serenity Wilson, who is actually a character from my first book. However, the poem was written by me.

Enjoy!

CaSaundra W. Foreman-Harris

CHAPTER ONE

The Funeral

The Lord is my shepherd I shall not want. He maketh me to lie down in green pastures. He leadeth me beside the still waters. He restoreth my soul. He leadeth me in the paths of righteousness for His name sake. Yeah, though I walk through the valley of the shadow of death, I will fear no evil. Thy rod and thy staff, they comfort me. Thou prepareth a table before me in the presence of mine enemies. Thou annointeth my head with oil. My cup runneth over. Surely goodness and mercy shall follow me all the days of my life. And I shall dwell in the house of the Lord, forever. —Amen.

It was cold and rainy that day in December.

As I stepped out of my gray Honda, onto the muddy surface, I could feel the wind race beneath my black skirt. My baby sister was still sitting in my car, trying to take another puff of her cigarette. I let my umbrella up, and the wind began to tug at it as the raindrops, which felt like ice, splashed against my face.

The others were now stepping out of their cars, with umbrellas extended. The fierce wind seemed to chase us, as it shadowed our footsteps up the hill.

As we made our way to the top of the hill, where the final resting place was, we stood close together, my sisters and I, trying to keep warm and dry.

There weren't very many people there, that morning on the hill. My three sisters, my father, my mother's sister, my mother's husband, myself and a handful of others were the only ones who'd turned out that cold, winter day to pay their last respects to our mother.

I can remember that there were no tears that day. I can remember that the minister spoke kind words of her. Words that were much kinder than any she'd ever spoken to us...her children.

CaSaundra W. Foreman-Harris

I recall looking around at each of my sisters. Blank stares claimed the expressions on their faces, as they fixed their eyes on our mother's coffin. I knew that each of them, as I, were thinking of a moment when our mother was alive…but not really a part of our lives.

A graveside service was all that her husband could afford. Her flowers, red roses and a few white carnations, had been sent by some of our friends. The wind made the petals of the flowers move as the raindrops began to form ice on the petals.

After the minister completed the service, I laid a red rose on my mother's coffin. I said a silent prayer, and a silent good-bye to the woman who had brought me into this world.

That evening, after the family had gathered for dinner at my aunt's house, I took the long way home. The route by the lake was what I needed to take my mind off the funeral.

As I drove, the beauty of the water made me smile for a moment. Then, in another moment, I thought of how my mother had left my sisters and I alone. And now, she was gone for good.

Two weeks after my mother's funeral, I still had not been able to cry. My husband said that I needed to. But, I didn't know what to cry for. Why should I cry for a woman who never loved me? Why should I cry for a woman who wasn't there to protect me? Why should I cry for a woman whose heart was as cold as the wind that blew through us on the day we buried her? Why should I cry for this woman who was only around for the first two and a half years of my life?

My mother, the woman who left three, helpless little girls, all alone on the steps of a convenience store, did not deserve my tears. My mother, whom I shall refer to as Helen throughout this story, was not worthy of my sympathy. (At least that was what I felt for a long time after her death.)

My name is Deanna, and this is my story.

The story of: *The Motherless Children*.

2

CHAPTER TWO

From the Beginning

Once upon a time, more specifically, in June of 1950, my mother, Helen Elizabeth Davis was born in a small town called Brownwood, Texas. Her mother and father lived in a shack-like house on a farm near the edge of town. My mother was the youngest girl. Her sister, Virginia, was two years older.

This is probably a good time to point out that Helen is white. Her father, I need to add, did not like black people.

Although Helen's mother never took part in the ignorant practice of bigotry, she didn't encourage her husband to stop.

Helen and her sister were beautiful little girls. And, as time went on, they became very beautiful young ladies.

Eventually, they began to sneak out of the house at night to sneak off to a small town down the road where kids from school hung out. There was a club there called Sugar's. That's where Helen met John Anderson, the man who would someday be my father.

Helen and John began to see each other often.

After a while, Helen and Virginia stopped going to the club because John and one of his friends would meet them at a secret place in town.

After about four months, Helen and John had become really close. Although she was only seventeen, John asked her to marry him.

Helen was afraid to ask her father if she could marry John because she knew how he felt about blacks. So she kept putting John off.

As the months went by, Helen realized that she was gaining weight. Her parents noticed it too.

She had missed a couple of periods, and had been nauseous, but didn't think much of it. She didn't think much of it, until the night she felt movement in her stomach. She was startled.

3

That same night, she sneaked out to meet John.

When she got to the special meeting place, John wasn't there. Helen waited for an hour. It wasn't like John to be late, and she was worried. All sorts of things were running through her mind. She wondered if he had changed his mind about meeting her. She wondered if he didn't want to see her anymore. She wondered if he was with someone else. She wondered if he'd been in an accident.

He had.

On John's way to their special meeting place, down by the creek, surrounded by oak trees, he had been followed by two white men in a blue pick-up truck. They tried to run his black Impala off the road. Finally, after about thirty-minutes of reckless driving, John's car ran into a tree. The two white men, believing he was dead, fled the scene, while John sat slumped over the steering wheel of the car, bleeding.

As Helen walked home from her disappointing evening, she noticed the headlights of a car ahead. As she walked closer, she recognized the car. It was John's.

Helen ran towards the black Impala, crumpled into the tree. She wondered if he was alive. She wondered if he was...dead.

As Helen reached the door of the car, she could see blood on John's head. His silhouette seemed lifeless in the darkness of the night. She called his name. He didn't answer.

For a moment, she stood there as if her feet were glued to the ground. She was speechless.

Movement in the tree behind her brought Helen to realize she needed to get help. She ran to the nearest house, but a big, black dog growled and began to bark at her. With tears streaming down her eyes, and fear in her heart, she ran to the next house. A light was on inside, so she knocked on the door. An old black man came to the door. He peered through the screen of the door. Seeing Helen, a white girl standing on his porch, the man opened the door cautiously.

"Sir, there has been an accident up the road. A man...my friend...his car hit a tree. He's hurt badly. Can you help him please?" she stammered.

"Just a minute, Sugar," the man said. He went back into the house and grabbed the keys to his truck. He came back out side. "You stay here, I'll bring your friend back," he said as he ran to his truck.

Helen, who still had tears streaming down her face, sat on the steps of the porch. She watched the old man in his old green pick-up truck race down the road. She watched the taillights of the pick-up truck for as long as she could see them. Then, they disappeared.

Suddenly, an elderly woman appeared at the door. She stared out at Helen through the screen door. "Come on in," she said.

Helen turned around. She hadn't realized there was anyone standing behind her.

The old woman repeated herself. "Come on in." She opened the screen door wide.

Helen was hesitant at first. She thought for a moment, then smiled at the woman standing in the doorway. She slowly walked over the threshold.

As Helen stepped into the living room, she noticed lots of pictures on the wall. Some of the pictures were of young men in army uniforms; another was of three little boys smiling while playing outdoors.

"Those are my sons. Triplets. Jeremiah, Joshua, and Jacob. They're all in the service," the woman said proudly. She gestured for Helen to have a seat on the plaid sofa. "What's your name, Sweetie?" the old woman asked, as she sat down on a matching plaid chair directly across from Helen.

"Helen. What's yours?"

"My name is Sister Sylvia. But most people call me Sister," she replied. After a few minutes of silence, Sister Sylvia said, "Well, Helen, how far along are you?"

"I'm not sure what you're talking about," Helen replied.

"How many months are you?"

"How many months?" Helen repeated. She had no clue what the old woman was talking about. What she did know was that this old woman was talking too much, and the old man was taking too long.

"Sugar, don't you know? You are with child. You are pregnant."

Helen almost fainted. Pregnancy had never entered her mind. She remembered the nausea and the missed periods, the weight gain...the trouble she was in.

She passed out.

When she came to, she was lying on the plaid sofa with a cool towel on her forehead. She could hear voices, one of which was John's. She got up off of the sofa and followed the sound of John's voice into the next room. On a bed in the corner lay John. The elderly woman was rubbing his forehead with a towel.

As Helen stood in the doorway of the bedroom, the floorboard squeaked.

Sister Sylvia turned to look at Helen. "Are you all right? You turned as white as a sheet, and then you passed out," she said.

"I'm fine Sister Sylvia. How's John?"

"He'll be alright, Honey. He's going to have an awful headache in the morning, but he's alright." She placed a bandage on his forehead and wiped the dried blood from around his right eye.

"Helen, what are you doing here?" John asked.

"That's not important right now. But I have to get home before my parents start to look for me." She turned to leave.

John made an attempt to get up, but he was dizzy and fell back to his seat.

"Young man, you don't need to try to move right now. You need to rest." Sister Sylvia scolded him.

"I've got to walk her home!" he said, struggling again to get to his feet.

6

"Bill, drive this young lady home. She shouldn't be out this time of night anyway. Considering her condition," the elderly woman said to her husband.

"What condition?" asked John.

Before Helen could answer, the elderly woman exclaimed, "She's pregnant!"

John sat straight up on the bed. He looked Helen up and down.

"Is that true?" he asked her.

Softly, Helen answered, "I'm really not sure." She focused her eyes on the worn brown carpet on the floor. Tears were forming in her eyes.

"Oh, there's no doubt about it, she's definitely pregnant. I can see it in her face, throat, breasts and hips. Looks to be about four or five months. And it's going to be a girl. I know that because I took this needle and string here, and placed it in front of her belly while she was passed out. Now, the way that string moved, it's definitely a girl!" Sister Sylvia walked over and placed her hand on Helen's stomach.

Embarrassed, and trying to avoid the discussion, Helen made another attempt to leave. "I've really got to get home."

The elderly gentleman followed her out, and walked her to his pick-up truck.

John stumbled to the door and yelled to her, "Meet me tomorrow night, okay!"

Helen looked at John and nodded her head. Then she and the old gentleman drove down the road, disappearing into the night.

When Helen crawled through her bedroom window that night, her room was dark. As she closed the window, the light suddenly came on. Helen turned around very slowly. Her father was sitting in the chair, beside the light switch. He sat there, with his arms folded, and the look on his face told her that she was in trouble.

Virginia lay in her bed, on the other side of the room pretending to be asleep.

"Helen Elizabeth! Where the hell have you been?"

"Uh, Daddy...I can explain. I...uh...I went to...the library. And then on the way back, I saw a car accident and I ran and got help. I lost track of the time because I was trying to make sure the man was all right." Helen knew that she was telling a half-truth, but hoped her father would believe her."

"Girl, do you think I was born yesterday?" her father screamed. His face was red, and the veins were popping out of the side of his neck...which was a definite indicator that Helen's story was not going to keep her out of trouble. "I heard that you been sneaking around with some nigger. Is that true?"

Taken by surprise, Helen couldn't look her father straight in the eyes. She lied, "No Daddy...I don't know what you're talking about."

Helen's dad got up from the rickety wooden chair and walked over to her by the window. For a moment, he stood there. He was getting madder by the minute. Then he raised his hand, and slapped her across the face.

"Don't lie to me girl! Just look at you. Word is that you are pregnant. Are you?"

"I don't know Daddy!"

He slapped her again. "Don't lie to me Helen. I see you gaining weight. Your mother says you've been throwing up. Who's the daddy?"

Helen didn't answer him.

Her father raised his hand to strike her again.

"Daddy, please don't hit her again! Please!" Virginia screamed. She jumped out of her bed and stepped in front of Helen. "Daddy, don't hit her. She's pregnant. But she doesn't know who the father is...because...she was raped!"

Helen's father stepped back.

"What? Raped? When?"

"Several months ago," Virginia continued to lie. "We were afraid to tell you because we didn't know how you would react."

8

"Helen...why didn't you tell me?" he asked, as he sat down on the bed. He was in shock at first. "Who did this to you? Was he a nigger?"

Helen still continued her silence. She didn't know how to lie as well as Virginia, and she looked to her for assistance. She wanted this moment to be over. She wanted her father out of her room.

"Daddy...Helen needs her rest," Virginia said.

"Okay," he said. "Helen, we'll finish this tomorrow. You get some rest now." He got up to leave the room. He turned again to look at her. "I'm sorry I hit you." Then he walked out of the room.

Helen's tears fell over the place where her father's hand hit her face. Her face was red and sore. Virginia had followed her father out of the room to get Helen some ice for her face.

That night Helen didn't sleep. She understood why Virginia lied for her, but she really would have preferred to tell her father the truth. The truth was that she'd been seeing a black man, had fallen in love with him, and was now pregnant with his baby; a baby that might come into the world with dark skin.

She held her tear soaked pillow tightly. It was her security; security in a world that was unkind and prejudice to the differences in people.

The next morning, Helen's father told her mother that she had been raped and was pregnant. They decided that the best thing for the family would be for her to go away and have the baby, and give it up for adoption.

That night Helen didn't meet John at their secret place. Her father had driven her to a town three hours away to stay in a home for pregnant girls.

As John sat in his friend's car that night, waiting for Helen, he decided to ask her to go away with him so they could get married, and raise their baby together.

Virginia sneaked out of the house that night. Helen had asked her to go meet John and tell him where she was.

When John saw Virginia, he knew something was wrong.

"Where's Helen?"

"My dad caught her sneaking in last night. He confronted her about being pregnant. We sort of made up a story about how she got pregnant. Anyway, earlier today he took her to a home for pregnant girls. When the baby is born…it will be put up for adoption."

John was crushed. He didn't know what to say.

"I've got to get back home. I'll try to find out where she is okay."

"Virginia, if you talk to her, tell Helen I love her."

"I will," she said. Then she turned and ran home.

Four months later, on November 10, 1967, Helen gave birth to a baby girl. She saw her baby for a brief moment before the baby was taken away. Helen knew that she would never forget this moment. The tiny, vanilla colored baby, with the caramel colored curls, would be a sight she would keep imbedded in her mind. Forever.

A few days after the baby was born, Helen caught a bus back to Brownwood. As she sat on the bus, she thought of John, and wondered if she would see him again. She thought about the beautiful baby girl that she'd given the name Faith. Although she knew that the birth of Faith was something she wouldn't be able to discuss again, she secretly hoped that someday she'd get to see her baby again.

Helen's return home was not what she'd expected.

From November to January, Helen was depressed. Her father barely spoke to her. Her mother seemed to avoid her. Virginia tried to help her feel better, but nothing seemed to help.

One night, Virginia talked Helen into going to the movies. Their father let them drive the car.

Once they made it to the drive-in, Virginia parked the Chevy in the back.

"Why are you parking all the way back here?" Helen asked her.

"No reason. Just watch the movie, and take it easy."

As the two sisters sat in the car, watching the movie and talking, a very familiar silhouette approached the car. It was a man. And, as the man walked up to the passenger side of the blue Chevy, Helen saw that the silhouette belonged to John.

CHAPTER THREE

The Thin, Tall, Black Man

For several months after Helen and John were reunited, they resumed their meetings at their special place.

Helen told him about the baby and her experience while she was away having their baby. John shared with her how he'd tried to find her, but was unsuccessful.

As the winter weather changed to spring, Helen once again found herself gaining weight and feeling nauseous.

One night in April, as they sat in his new car down by the creek, she told John that she was pregnant again. He told her not to worry, and that he would take care of everything.

Helen wasn't quite sure what he meant by that, but she liked the sound of it. After going through the last pregnancy alone, she felt safe and reassured that this time, the man she loved would be with her.

As he stroked her arm, John turned to look Helen in the eyes. "Helen, we need to go away. We need to go someplace where we can be together...openly...and raise our baby."

"Okay John, but how? When?" she asked, while he held her close to his heart. She could feel his heart racing faster with each breath.

"I don't know. But I'll think of something."

About a week after their conversation, John showed up at Helen's house.

When Helen's mother answered the door, John politely said, "Mrs. Davis, is your husband home?"

Helen's mother was surprised that a black man was standing at her doorstep. No black person had ever knocked on the Davis' door before.

"I'm sorry...but...umm...Mr. Davis isn't here right now. And...I have to warn you, even if he was, he probably wouldn't talk to you. He...he...he...doesn't like coloreds."

John was a bit taken back by Mrs. Davis' honesty.

"Well, Mrs. Davis, that's okay, because...I'm not colored, I'm black. Now, I really need to speak with him." John insisted. He could tell that Mrs. Davis was nervous by his presence.

"Sir, you'd better go now," she said, as she closed the door in his face.

John went back to his car. He sat for a moment thinking of how to talk to this man about his daughter...the daughter that he had impregnated twice. But, John loved her. So, he felt that he had to do this for her sake, as well as his own.

Later that evening, right before dark, John went back to Helen's house. As he pulled into the yard, he noticed a white truck parked close to the house. That truck wasn't there earlier. John began to sweat.

As John walked up the steps to the front door, he heard a commotion going on inside the house. He heard a man's loud voice...he heard a scream. Then, he heard Helen screaming, "Daddy don't!"

John knocked on the door. He knew that something strange was going on inside that house.

Mr. Davis came to the door. He was surprised to see a tall, thin black man standing there.

"What the hell do you want?" he snapped. The red faced, fat white man, in his blue-jean overalls wasn't quite what John expected.

"Uh, sir, I came to talk with you about Helen." John was so nervous.

"Helen? We don't have anything to talk about," her father said. He reached behind the door and made visible a twelve-gauge shotgun.

John kept his cool. He placed his hand in his back pocket, where he was carrying a small pistol.

"Well, Sir, there's no easy way to say this, but Helen and I have been seeing each other. And I would like to ask you if I can marry her." John could see the color drain from Helen's

13

father's face. He saw the man's fingers tighten up around the barrel of his gun.

"What you can do, nigger, is get the hell off of my property before I kill you." He opened the screen door and stepped outside, onto the porch.

"Sir, I'm sorry, but I can't leave without Helen. She's pregnant with my child, and I want to marry her!"

Without warning, bullets began to fly from the white man's gun. One of them hit John in his right leg. Instantly, reflex took over, and John pulled his pistol from his back pocket and aimed it at Mr. Davis' heart. He didn't miss. The white man fell on the porch. Blood was everywhere.

Helen's mother appeared at the door.

"Travis! Travis!" she yelled, as she quickly ran to her husband's side. She cradled him in her arms. "Say something to me!"

In a voice filled with hatred, the man told his wife, "Betty, pick up my gun and kill that nigger!"

Before Helen's mother had a chance to pick up the gun, Virginia picked it up off of the ground.

"Virginia! What are you doing?" her father yelled.

"I'm setting Helen free," she said. "She needs to be with him so they can raise their baby together."

"You knew that she was seeing that...that nigger?" her father asked. He was bleeding profusely.

Just as Virginia was about to answer, Helen bolted out of the house with a suitcase.

"Where are you going?" her mother asked.

"Wherever John's going. It doesn't matter, as long as we are together."

Helen ran to John, who was limping to his car. She opened the passenger side door for him, and helped him get in the car.

"If you leave with him today, don't you ever come back!" her father shouted. "Nigger, if I ever see you again, I'll kill you!"

Nervously, Helen got in the car on the driver's side. She started the ignition. For a moment, her mother's eyes met hers. She could see the helplessness in her mother's facial expression.

Just as she put the car in drive, Virginia ran out to the black Impala to hug her sister good-bye.

"Keep in touch, okay," Virginia said, still holding her father's gun in one hand, and her sister's hand in the other.

Helen stopped at the nearest hospital. While she was waiting for John to be seen in the emergency room, an ambulance arrived. She heard the doctor's in the waiting room talking. There was a lot of hospital jargon that Helen didn't understand. But she had no problem understanding the term D.O.A.

Helen heard a familiar sob. It was her mother's.

Travis Davis died on the way to the hospital. The bullet that killed him belonged to a thin, tall black man, who had gotten his daughter pregnant.

CHAPTER FOUR

Baby Boom!

As the leaves blanketed yards everywhere, the changes of the season brought about the birth of Helen and John's second child.

Angel Marie Anderson was born October 2, 1968 in Mullin, Texas. John and Helen settled there because one of John's brothers got him a job at a factory.

Money was tight, but Helen and John managed to make ends meet. They lived in a little house that had one bedroom, one bathroom and a kitchen, combined with a den. They rented the house furnished, although the furniture looked like something somebody threw away, and so did the house. It was the best they could do.

Helen wanted a new baby bed for Angel, who was given her name because Helen felt that Angels had watched over she and John and kept them safe from harm and danger. So, John worked overtime to give her whatever she asked for.

In January of 1969, Helen realized that she was pregnant again. She had been sick, but thought it was a stomach virus. John made her go to the doctor so that she wouldn't make Angel sick.

When she realized that she was pregnant, she felt a bit discouraged because she knew that money was tight and times were already hard.

Helen waited almost two weeks before she told John. His reaction was joyful. He told her that he had always wanted a big family.

"Baby," he said, as he got down on one knee in front of her, "don't worry yourself about anything. I love you, and I will take care of you. As a matter of fact, I've been thinking about us a lot lately. I've been thinking about us getting married. What do you think?"

Helen was surprised by the conversation. The two had discussed getting married someday, but the day never really crossed her mind.

"Well, I guess now would be just as good a time as any," she said, with a smile.

On February 14, 1969, John, Helen and Angel stood before Reverend Edzell Scott in the little white church at the edge of town, and before God and John's family, exchanged wedding vows.

In March, John and Helen were able to move into a two-bedroom house in a nicer part of town. On the outside, the house was white stucco, with a white picket fence around the whole house. On the inside, the walls were white in every room, except in the bathroom, where the walls were green. The house had hard wood floors, and lots of windows. John's boss owned the house, and charged them a minimal amount of rent.

Helen was happy in her new home, and John was glad. He enjoyed making her happy. He enjoyed seeing her smile.

To earn extra money, Helen baby-sat for the neighbors. She'd charge them twenty dollars a week.

On September 23, 1969, Helen gave birth to JaLeesa Virginia Anderson. John was just as proud of this baby girl, who had light brown hair, as he was of Angel.

Although he never told Helen, he was overwhelmed with the bills. And, it was during that time he began to drink, and hang out with his buddies after work.

Then, the arguments began. Helen couldn't understand why John couldn't come home after work and spend time with her and the babies. On the other hand, John couldn't understand why she was complaining.

By December, John began to stay out later, and later. When he did decide to finally come home, he was so drunk that he couldn't see, or walk straight.

Helen had grown more and more frustrated. Eventually, her inability to cope with her marriage led her to call her sister,

Virginia, who was still living in Brownwood, to come pick her up.

On December 20th, an extremely cold day, Helen packed her things while John was at work. She'd made arrangements for Virginia to come to the house while John was away.

"Aren't you going to tell John you're leaving?" Virginia asked her sister, while loading three suit cases, a diaper bag and a small white box into her 1967 pink Cadillac.

"No, Virginia, I'm not. Sometimes, you've got to make a man realize what he has. And, sometimes, a man doesn't realize what he has, until it's gone. I've been trying to talk to him for months. He just doesn't listen. I am tired of spending all of my time with these kids, by myself," she explained. Tears rolled down Helen's cheeks, as they pulled out of the driveway of the pretty, little white stucco house, with the white picket fence, and the pretty green grass.

When John crawled into the bed at 2:00 a.m., December 21, he reached over to hug Helen. But, she wasn't there.

He sat up in the bed, and turned on the lamp beside him. He was puzzled. "Helen," he called out. She didn't answer.

John got out of bed, and went to the bedroom that Angel and JaLeesa shared. There were no precious baby girls, with curly brown hair and rosy red cheeks, sleeping in the white cribs along the walls.

Dazed, and confused, John walked back into his room and opened the closet door. After turning on the light, he ran his fingers across the empty clothes racks that hung on the rod inside the closet; the empty racks that Helen hung her clothes on.

It was then, that he knew he had messed up.

His wife had left him, and taken the babies.

John walked over to the bed and sat down. With his head in his hands, he thought about the things she'd been trying to tell him for months. Now, it was too late. Two hours had passed since John first realized that Helen was gone.

He sat in the living room in the big brown recliner Helen had bought him for his birthday. Staring at the TV, and smoking cigarettes, he thought back to when they first met, and the times they shared at their secret place.

He missed his wife. He missed his little girls.

His mind drifted back to his childhood, and the day his own mother had left his father.

John was only four-years old, that cold night in January of 1953, when his mother, with her three babies, walked through the snow to the bus station.

His mind recalled the awful fight that had transpired between his parents, which resulted in a physical confrontation. His mother ended up with a black eye, and his father ended up with a broken nose.

That night, as a child, he promised himself that he would never hit his wife, and that he would never be away from his children. After that fight between his parents, John never saw his father again.

At five o'clock in the morning, John called his job and told them he wouldn't be in. He told them he had a family emergency.

By nine o'clock that same morning, John was in Brownwood, sitting in front of Helen's mother's house. As he sat in the car, he recalled the last time he'd sat in that driveway...the day he'd shot Helen's father.

Unsure of how upset Helen was with him, he took his time getting out of the car. He shut the car door quietly behind him and then leaned his twenty-year-old frame against the car. Reluctantly, he shoved his hands into his pockets, and took baby steps toward the front door of the house where his wife had grown up. He knocked on the door.

"Who is it?" asked a voice from the inside.

"John Anderson," he answered, in his deep, alto voice. Helen came to the door and opened it a little.

"What are you doing here?" she asked, with an attitude. She opened the door a tad bit wider, but didn't unhook the screen door.

"Baby, I came to apologize, and ask you to come back home with me. I promise you, that I'll stop staying out late drinking. I'll be a better husband, and a better father. Baby, please come home…" he pleaded with her.

Although she was angry, Helen could tell he was sincere. However, she felt like he needed to sweat a little more.

"What makes you think that I believe you'll stop coming home late, and drinking all night with your friends?"

"Helen, have I ever lied to you before?"

"No," she answered, softly.

"Well, then, my word is the only thing I have that I can give and keep at the same time. Now, baby, you know I love you. And, I just forgot myself for a moment. I'm young…and foolish…but I know what's right. And, Baby, what's right is you, and me, and Angel, and JaLessa; a family in our own home."

Helen looked at him through the screen door. Her arm slowly reached up towards the latch on the screen door. As she unhooked it, Angel began to cry inside the house.

"Come in, John," she said, as she turned to check on Angel.

By April of 1970, Helen was pregnant, again. John was still working at the factory. By that time, he had gotten a promotion, but with two babies still in diapers, money was tight; even with Helen babysitting for the neighbors.

On October 5, 1970, at 11:09 a.m., Helen gave birth to Mariah Diana Anderson. This was not a happy occasion…Mariah died twenty-one hours later from complications of a premature birth.

John was crushed.

Helen seemed relieved.

For the next year, John and Helen argued about birth control.

Helen had decided that she didn't want to have any more children. She felt that two little girls were enough, and wanted to get her tubes tied.

John on the other hand, felt they were too young to make that decision. He had his sights set on fathering a son. Therefore, Helen getting her tubes tied was definitely out of the question.

On August 2, 1973, I, Deana Nicole Anderson, was born. I was the fifth daughter of John and Helen Anderson.

Girls! Girls! Girls!

Eventually, Helen brought up the subject of getting her tubes tied again. She didn't want any more babies, and to her, it seemed unlikely that after having five girls (she always included their first baby that was given up for adoption) that she would be able to give John a son.

John, however, persuaded Helen to try one more time. "This time, even if it's not a boy, you can get your tubes tied."

In July of 1974, Helen realized that she was pregnant again, and she was praying for a boy.

With this last pregnancy, Helen had complications. She was tired all of the time, and extremely sick. In October, three months into her pregnancy, she began to experience severe cramping in her stomach. Her back hurt all of the time, and her feet were always swollen.

By the middle of November, the doctor restricted Helen to bed rest. Her sister volunteered to stay with them and help out until the baby was born.

Early on the morning of February 12, 1975, Helen got up to go to the bathroom and noticed that she was bleeding. She wasn't in any pain, but she knew that bleeding was a bad sign. Even more frightening than the blood was the fact that the baby wasn't moving around inside of her.

"John," she screamed, "we've got to go to the hospital. Something's wrong. I'm bleeding!"

Calmly, John said to his wife, "Don't worry Helen. Everything will be alright." He helped her get dressed, then picked her up and carried her to the car.

By the time they reached the hospital, Helen had begun to have labor pains.

"I've had five babies, and none of them ever hurt this bad," she said to John, as she winced at the pain.

John held her hand and tried to comfort her.

Once they were in the emergency room, the doctor told Helen that she was dilated to a six.

"It's too soon!" John said. "The baby isn't due until April! What's going on?"

The doctor told John that the baby was having some complications, and would be born prematurely.

After six hours of labor, Helen gave birth to Jazmine Anderson, who weighed three pounds, four ounces. The nurses took Jazmine, whose cry was very weak, to run tests on her. Her lungs were not fully developed, and her left hand…only had two fingers, and a thumb.

Helen was hysterical. She didn't understand what she had done wrong.

John was overcome by his emotions as well. He knew that there was nothing he could do to change things for this beautiful little girl with curly chestnut brown hair. He felt bad because all throughout Helen's pregnancy, he'd prayed for a boy, instead of praying for a healthy baby.

When Helen was released from the hospital, Jazmine stayed for six more weeks. It was a requirement that she weigh at least four pounds, and have the ability to digest milk before being allowed to go home.

During that time, Helen was deeply depressed. She wouldn't eat or come out of her room. The doctor told John that it was normal for women to go through depression after having a baby. However, John believed Helen's state of depression was serious. She wouldn't play with her other children, nor would she go to the hospital to see Jazmine.

Virginia and John took turns at the hospital feeding Jazmine, while neighbors and friends helped with the three other Anderson children.

The second week in April, the doctor released Jazmine from the hospital.

Virginia put a banner up in the living room that read, "Welcome Home Jazmine" and baked a cake to celebrate. She was really excited when she told Angel, who was six-years-old, JaLeesa, who was five-years-old and myself, who was almost two-years-old, that our baby sister was finally coming home.

That day, Helen tried to pretend that she was okay as John placed Jazmine in her arms. But she wasn't.

She never let her eyes look past Jazmine's face, and she never allowed Jazmine's blanket to reveal what she was ashamed of...the flaw of her left hand.

CHAPTER FIVE

Dropped Off...

The birth of baby Jazmine was a major turning point for our family.

Her handicap was a daily stress factor for Helen. She just wasn't able to cope with having a daughter who wasn't perfect. She felt as though she had done something wrong, and was being punished by God.

John tried to reassure her that Jazmine was okay, and perfect...despite the fact that her hand wasn't completely formed. He told Helen that God was not punishing her for anything she'd done wrong. He tried to encourage Helen to see the positive view, instead of the negative, which was that they had been blessed with a beautiful little girl.

By June of 1975, Helen had lost all of her motherly joy and charm. She was always cranky and never wanted to hold Jazmine. Angel and JaLessa became Jazmine's babysitter because Helen felt as though they were big enough to look after her. I was still a baby myself, almost two-years old, but Helen didn't choose to nurture any of us...her children...her little girls.

John worked long hours. From six o'clock in the morning, until two o'clock in the afternoon, he worked at the factory. He would come home after work, spend time with us (his girls), cook our dinner, wash clothes, read us stories, bathe us, and tuck us into bed. Around eight o'clock, he'd sleep for a couple of hours. Then at ten o'clock, he'd wake up and prepare himself to go to his second job, in which he worked from eleven o'clock at night, until four o'clock in the morning stocking groceries at a local supermarket.

John began to get tired of putting forth so much effort, while Helen did nothing.

One Tuesday morning in September, John came home at two o'clock in the afternoon to find that Helen had left my sisters and

I alone. He was angry, but tried not to let us see how upset he was.

Helen didn't come home that night, or the next night either. John called Virginia in Brownwood, but she had not seen or heard from Helen.

John had gotten an elderly lady who lived across the street to look after us while he went to work.

Finally, after two days, Helen came home. When she walked in the house, she went straight to her bedroom and closed the door. She didn't hug any of us, or even acknowledge the presence of the old lady.

When John got home from work that day, he could tell by the look on the old lady's face that something wasn't right. "What's wrong, Miss Jerrel?" he asked, as he walked over to the door which lead into the bedroom my sisters and I shared. "Is something wrong with one of the kids?"

The old lady shook her head, and in a very quiet voice, almost like a whisper, she said, "Your wife came home today. She's in your bedroom."

John stood still for a moment, not sure he heard the old lady correctly, John said, "I'm sorry...I didn't understand what you said."

Miss Jerrel frowned, as she repeated herself.

John turned and looked towards his bedroom door. Slowly, he turned and walked the five steps from our bedroom to his. He stood there for a moment. Then, he turned the doorknob, and pushed the door open. Helen was lying across the bed, with her nightgown on. For another moment, John stood in the doorway, not quite sure what to say or how to say it. Then, he closed the door behind him.

For a while, there were no sounds coming from behind the white door, with the peeling paint. But the sound of silence didn't last very long. Raised voices...Words we weren't aloud to repeat...The sound of a hand hitting flesh...The sound of glass shattering against the floor. The sound of struggling so intense, it was hard to believe we weren't watching a movie on TV.

25

Then the door opened, and John, walking backwards barely escaped the flying shoe that was aimed at his head.

"I want you out. And I want you out now!" she shouted, as she finally emerged from the bedroom.

"I'm not leaving without my kids," he told her, as he shielded his face from another swinging hand.

"Your kids?" she said. "Well, you can take Jazmine, but the rest of them stay with me!" She had her hand on her hip, and was rolling her neck. She was looking really bad. I recall her hair being wild, and her nightgown being ripped. I recall a small red scratch on her right forearm, and a bright red bruise on her cheek. I recall smeared makeup.

John wasn't surprised that Helen was willing to give up Jazmine so easily, and he had no problem with taking her. However, he was reluctant to leave the rest of us.

"How are you going to take care of yourself and these kids, Helen?"

"Don't worry about us. We'll be fine!" she yelled at him.

By Christmas of 1975, John had decided to move to Waco, Texas where he had been offered a better job. His sister also lived there, and would help him with Jazmine. Even though Helen wouldn't allow him to see my sisters and me, John would leave money for her each week in the mailbox. Times were really rough. Some days, Helen would leave the house early in the morning, and tell Angel to watch us.

Angel had to cook for us, and clean the house, and she made JaLeesa help her.

On Christmas Day, John came to the house with lots of presents for us. Helen, who was asleep when he came, didn't know that he had been there. She slept through the whole day.

That day, he told my sisters and me that he and Jazmine were moving away. Angel begged him to take us with him. Although saddened by my sister's pleas and tears, John said that he couldn't take us right then, but that he would come back for us as soon as he could.

My sisters and I spent the month of January 1976 trying to stay warm. Helen had not paid the electric bill, so the house was cold. Helen stayed gone all of the time. My sisters and I began to appreciate the times when she was gone.

February and March came, and went. Helen had begun to bring strange men into our home. Then the electricity started to work again, and there was food to eat. And, Helen seemed happy, or at least giggly all of the time.

By May, Helen had grown tired of having us around. The Social Services people had begun to stop by our house almost everyday to inquire about Angel and JaLeesa not being in school. Helen would lie about their ages. One day, one of the Social workers came to our house with copies of birth certificates that proved my sisters real ages.

Helen didn't know what to do. She couldn't let Angel and JaLeesa go to school because there would be no one to watch me. Besides, it was too late for them to attend school anyway; school would be out in June.

On the second Saturday in May, Helen dressed us all in our best clothes. She even took the time to put bows and ribbons in our hair.

Angel asked her where she was taking us.

Helen looked at her, then smiled and said, "To see your daddy."

Later that morning, after a two-hour long drive in Helen's newest boyfriend's car, we arrived in Waco, Texas.

Helen told her boyfriend that she wanted to find a park. So, he drove to a place called Cameron Park. I remember seeing lots of trees, and winding roads. I remember being afraid because Helen's boyfriend drove around the curves as if he were on some sort of carnival ride.

"Okay, everybody, let's get out. Mommy wants to take some pictures of you girls. You look so pretty." She pulled out a pocket-sized camera and handed it to Ellis, her boyfriend. She then proceeded to position us in a line in front of a big, rock wall. She stood behind us, and told Ellis to take our picture. After that, we got back into the car and drove some more.

I recall my sisters and I kept eyeing one another. I remember Angel reaching over and putting her arm around me. I recall JaLessa laying her head on Angel's shoulder. We were afraid and unsure of what was about to happen. It just didn't seem right.

Even though I was a little girl, I can remember seeing a lot of trees and big houses as we rode around for what seemed like an hour before we finally pulled up at a neighborhood store. Suddenly, the car came to a stop.

Helen gave Angel two-dollars and told us to go into the store to buy something to drink. As Angel helped me out of the car, I remember hearing a man on the radio singing… *"Well it was just my imagination, running away with me…"*

Once we got to the door of the store, Helen got back in the car and yelled out the window, "You girls wait here. Your daddy will be here to get you soon." Then, she drove off, leaving three little girls (Angel, who was seven, JaLeesa, who was five, and me, Deanna who was two) alone on the steps of a neighborhood store.

Angel, with tears in her eyes, opened the door of the store and told us to follow her. JaLessa held my hand, as we followed closely on Angel's heels. She walked to the back of the store, past the candy and chip aisle, past the bread and pastry aisle, and slid the door open to the soda cooler. She pulled out two cans of Red soda and one Grape soda. Then she walked up to the counter and handed the man behind the counter a dollar. "Sir," she said, "do you know a man named John Anderson?"

The Hispanic man behind the counter, with a red buttoned-down shirt on, looked down at the three of us. He walked from behind the counter and took a pack of tissues off one of the shelves and handed one of the tissues to Angel. "Here sweetheart, wipe your eyes. Why are you crying?"

Angel dried her eyes, as much as possible.

"Our mother just dropped us off and said that our dad was going to come and get us. We don't know where we are, and I don't really believe that my dad does either." More tears began to fall.

The man took another tissue and handed it to Angel. He put his hand on her shoulder and told her not to worry, and that he'd see what he could do about finding our dad.

Eventually, the man told us his name was Rudy. He told Angel to get whatever we wanted off of the shelves to eat. Then he took us in the back of the store where there was a TV and a couch.

"You little ladies sit back here and make yourselves comfortable. I'll call around. I think I know your daddy. There's a man who's been in the store a few times with a little girl who looks a great deal like the three of you."

"That's our baby sister Jasmine!" JaLeesa said, while smiling and eating chips at the same time.

About seven o'clock that night, eight hours after Helen dropped us off, John came to pick us up. He was happy to see us, but upset because Helen had not told him that she was bringing us to stay with him. In fact, John had not spoken with Helen in over five months.

CHAPTER SIX

Daddy's Little Girls

I can remember riding down a street in daddy's black car. It was a hot summer day; two weeks after Helen abandoned us at the store. There were lots of big trees on this street, and almost every house on the street was white.

Slowly, the car came to a stop in front of a white house with navy blue shutters. The house was the biggest one I'd ever seen. Although the paint had cracks in it, it was still pretty. There were three big trees in the front yard, and beautiful green grass. From where we sat parked in the car, we could see a fence in the backyard.

"Who lives here?" Angel asked.

"We do," John replied. There was a big grin on his face. "This is our new home."

My sister and I looked at each other. Then we looked at him.

"Well, don't just sit there. Get out of the car and let's go see your new rooms."

Once inside the front door of the house John gave us a tour. There was a kitchen, a den, a bathroom and three bedrooms.

"Are Daddy's little girl's happy? Does everyone like our new home?" John asked, while holding Jazmine and me in his arms.

We shook our heads, signifying that we liked the house.

By September of that year, John had gotten Angel and JaLessa ready for school, and me and Jazmine ready for daycare. My sisters often talked about how excited they were because he'd taken us shopping for new school clothes.

The first day of school, John drove to one of the biggest buildings we'd ever seen. He walked each of my sisters to their class and told them to be good. He told them that he would be there to pick them up when school was out. Then, John drove Jazmine and me to daycare.

That evening, after school, my sisters and I came home to find a giant fish aquarium in the living room. The aquarium had tiny blue rocks at the bottom, and lots of green plastic plants. There was also a mermaid and an octopus at the bottom of the aquarium. Dozens of black mollies were the fish John had chosen to inhabit the most beautiful scene I'd ever viewed.

I recall being mesmerized by the life that consumed the glass box in front of me.

About the beginning of November, John began seeing a woman named Ruby. Ruby was tall and thin, the color of caramel, and had long hair. After only two weeks, she seemed to have moved herself into our home. At first, she appeared to be nice. She bought us cute dresses and combed our hair, which was a job that Angel had taken on.

Thanksgiving Day, Helen called to tell John she wanted a divorce. He told her to pay for it, but he was keeping his little girls. Helen had no intentions of trying to take us from him.

For Christmas that year, John bought us lots of toys. I specifically remember Santa Claus leaving me a brown baby doll with lots of curly hair and rosy cheeks. She wore a red and white polka dot dress, with matching panties. I named her Tina, after John's favorite singer, Tina Turner. That was the Christmas I remember the most.

As February approached, Ruby had become so cruel to us, that we spent a lot of time in our room. She treated Jasmine the worst. Angel, who was very stubborn, had turned eight in October. She and Ruby seemed to clash about everything, and this made things hard for the rest of us.

"Daddy's little girls," she said one day. "You spoiled brats may be your daddy's little girls, but you are not mine. He might let you get away with everything now, but that's going to change real soon."

One night, John came home early. As he quietly entered the house, he heard Ruby, yelling obscenities at Angel.

"You stupid little b—, I told you to clean up that kitchen. You are so lazy…probably just like your mother."

John quietly crept up behind Ruby. "Angel, go wash your face baby," he said to my sister who was standing in the kitchen crying. "Ruby, no one talks to my little girls like that. NO ONE! Cleaning up that kitchen is your responsibility. I'm taking care of my girls and you. You are responsible for cleaning this house and helping look after my girls. Now as for being lazy…how dare you call *her lazy*. She's a little girl, and…she does more for my girls than you do! And, then you were putting down my children's mother…you went a little too far. I trusted you to look after them and be kind to them. And yes, I know how you yell at them…I've also noticed how you mistreat Jazmine. So, in the best interest of my little girls, get your things, and get out!"

"But John, where am I supposed to go?"

"I don't know, and frankly I don't care. I do, however, care about Angel, JaLessa, Deanna and Jazmine. Therefore, as long as they have a place to live, I'm happy." As he turned away from Ruby, he saw our four little frames standing in the living room behind the sofa.

"Girls, go and put your shoes on. We're going for a ride," he said, while managing a smile.

As we turned to go to our room, I heard our father say to Ruby, "I want you gone when we get back."

That night, when we returned home, Ruby, the tall, thin, caramel colored, wicked witch was gone.

CHAPTER SEVEN

A Visit from Virginia

For almost two years, our lives with John seemed normal. We'd heard from Helen a couple of times, but we hadn't seen her since the day she left us alone at the store.

The Christmas of 1979, strange things began to happen.

Angel was eleven, JaLessa was ten, I was six and Jasmine was four.

John wasn't seeing anyone in particular, but he had begun to drink a lot. I think it had something to do with his job laying him off. To put food on the table, John got a job as a maintenance man at one of the elementary schools during the day, and cleaned buildings for a few hours at night. He hated it, but did it for us.

Some of his friends had begun to hang out around our house a lot…drinking and watching TV. Sometimes, John would drink himself to sleep.

Each day while John was working, a friend of his named Bryan would stop by. The week before Christmas, he brought presents wrapped in pretty, shiny packages with red and green bows on them to our house. He put the presents under our Christmas tree, which was covered with red satin balls and some gold colored bows. Angel peeked, when he wasn't looking, and saw that there was one present for each of us.

Uncle Bryan was what we called him. He was kind and made us laugh. JaLeesa thought he was handsome, and had a crush on him. She said he was the most beautiful, bald, yellow man she had ever seen. John would get him to check on us when he knew he'd be working late. Everyday he helped us with our homework.

JaLeesa, who hated school, always seemed to have so much homework. Every evening, she'd cry about how much she hated school. Bryan would always say to us, "Pretty, little ladies, don't you know a mind is a terrible thing to waste?"

I always thought he sounded like a parrot, mimicking the man from the television commercial.

The day before Christmas, John got sick and had to be rushed to the hospital. The doctor said it was a stomach ulcer, and told him to take it easy for a couple of days.

On Christmas day, Uncle Bryan and his wife came over to help John with us and cook dinner. Bryan's wife, Lori, let us help her in the kitchen, but we were more interested in playing with our new toys.

Shortly after dinner, there was a knock at the door. Helen's sister, Virginia, had come for a visit. It had been a long time since we'd seen her, but she still looked the same.

I remember she and John whispering about something in the living room, and then she came into our room to talk to us.

"Hey, how would you like to come spend a week with me? Your dad could really use a break right now." She looked at us with a smirk on her face. Her eyebrows were perfectly arched, and her hot-pink lipstick perfectly outlined her lips.

Angel, who was our spokesperson, looked at Aunt Virginia and said, "Our father doesn't need a break. He needs for me to help him, and help take care of my sisters."

A few days later, Child Protective Services showed up at our house. They said that they had received a complaint stating that we were living in a filthy house and that we weren't being taken care of.

As the social worker walked through our house, which was clean, and looked at us, who were happy and clean, she had no choice but to declare her report a false one.

John said it was Virginia who made that report because she was upset that we wouldn't go with her.

CHAPTER EIGHT

Not M, But C & E

Jesus.
God.
The Bible.
Religion.
My sisters and I didn't go to church very much when we were growing up. We were apart of that group people called CME's. You know, Christmas, Mother's Day and Easter. However, we didn't attend church on Mother's Day, just Christmas and Easter.

When we were little, John's sister, our Aunt Maya, would buy us dresses at Christmas and Easter. Angel and JaLeesa would get matching dresses, and Jazmine and I would get matching dresses.

My favorite Easter dress was the one I got when I was eight. It was white with purple and green flowers embroidered into the fabric. I remember twirling around and around because the dress flared out when I spun around. I also remember that my aunt fixed my hair in dozens of spiral curls. I felt so pretty that day.

Of course, by us only attending church on Christmas, and Easter, for along time, until I took it upon myself to read the Bible, I only knew two stories in the Bible. The first story being the birth of Jesus, whom we knew was born in a manger, and the second story being the crucifixion and resurrection of Jesus.

As I grew up, I often asked John why we only attended church on holidays. He would always say that he worked on Sundays and was only off on the holidays.

I don't know for sure that John worked every Sunday, but I do know that up until I was about twelve-years old, John was gone every Sunday morning. He'd come home about 11:30 am. Almost immediately after entering the house, John would check on the roast he had in the oven. He'd then add potatoes and carrots. The aroma was so intense that we could smell that roast all through the house.

Angel was in charge of making cornbread and JaLeesa was in charge of the tea. Jazmine and I were responsible for setting the table (and washing the dishes). We always said our blessing before we ate.

So, even though we didn't go to church every Sunday, my sisters and I did have a set routine for Sunday dinner.

John made Sundays seem special, just the way he made us feel.

As we grew older, by older I mean teenagers, my sisters and I would sometimes go to church with our Aunt Maya, or the lady next door. I enjoyed church, as did JaLeesa and Jazmine. Angel, however, chose to attend only on Christmas and Easter.

CHAPTER NINE

Emotions

Helen didn't bother to call us on our birthdays, or at Christmas. Mother's day came and went for us, as if it weren't even a holiday. None of us mentioned her, and neither did John. We were all quite content with the knowledge that our mother, the woman who birthed us, did not want us. None of us forgot the day she told our father to leave and take Jazmine with him, or the day she dropped us off at the store, like puppies abandoned by a careless, heartless owner. None of us longed for her. None of us spoke her name. None of us drew her image on our family pictures at school. None of us forgave her for the way she abandoned us.

Sometimes, when John would play music, and the song...*Just My Imagination*, by the Temptations would be on, I would have flashbacks to that day in May. I could recall the look on her face...that blue and white plaid dress she wore...even the scent of her cologne...as she drove away, waving...knowing she'd never come back. Like the lyrics to the song, I wondered if it was just my imagination, running away with me. I mean, who would imagine that a woman, a mother, would abandon her own daughters? Who would imagine that a woman, a mother, would never call to check on her daughters, or come by to say hello? Who would imagine that a woman, a mother, would not want to know how her daughters were growing into womanhood? However hard to believe, this was reality, and not my imagination. My sisters and I were motherless children; children without a mother. We had all come to the realization at an early age that John was the only parent we had, and he was as good as he could be.

Helen's absence from our lives affected each of us differently, although none of us ever really talked about it. I'm quite sure had she been a part of our lives on a more ordinary basis, our lives would have turned out slightly different. I'm almost positive that the emptiness we carried in our hearts would not have been there if Helen had cared for us and treated us with some sort of respect and love.

Although people say that they do not care whether or not someone cares about them, from experience, I can tell you that deep down inside, they really do. It's human nature, the desire we have to want to be loved, or feel loved by our parents, our mates, our children, and even our friends. For many years, I told myself that I didn't care about Helen. Yet, it wasn't long before I realized that I was fooling myself. I felt sorry for her.

My sisters and I were pretty much on our own in trying to figure out what role our gender played in life. We had no female role model to pattern after, and therefore had to pretty much make things up as we went along.

Many mistakes were made along the way. Sometimes, those mistakes made us mature. Sometimes, those mistakes made us strong. Sometimes, those mistakes made us cry. However, each mistake taught us something...

CHAPTER TEN

Angel

Men come easy for Angel because she is so beautiful. Yet just as easily as they come, they leave.

It's the wrong kind of men who are attracted to Angel. Some have been abusive, others drug pushers, drug users, alcoholics and jailbirds.

At the age of thirty-one, Angel is the mother of three; two boys and one girl. She isn't married, nor does she have a steady job. Her support comes from her live in boyfriend and AFDC, which she uses to pay her rent and bills. A low-income housing project is where she lives.

Angel didn't graduate from high school, nor did she get her G.E.D. She got pregnant when she was sixteen.

John didn't get upset when he found out Angel was pregnant, because of the things he and Helen had gone through. But when John found out that Angel was pregnant by one of his friends, a forty-seven-year-old man that he had always trusted around his daughters, he almost had a heart attack.

I remember John leaving the house with his pistol that night. His sister had taken Angel to the doctor, and she was the one who held Angel's hand while she told John.

John didn't shoot Uncle Bryan, the man who'd been having sex with Angel since she was thirteen. But a few days later Uncle Bryan was found dead floating in the river.

Angel continued to take care of us, and her son Donte.

When Angel turned eighteen, John moved out of the house and in with his new girlfriend.

We were all in our teens then, so John felt it would be okay to let us stay in the house alone, while he moved just two houses down from us.

By the time Angel turned nineteen she was pregnant again. When she told the guy who was the father of the baby, he beat her up…causing her to miscarry. Incidentally, this was the beginning of a long cycle of physical abuse Angel endured through the years.

At the age of twenty, Angel once again found herself in a relationship with an older man. His name was Easy Money.

Easy Money was always at our house. John didn't like him because he'd heard that Easy Money was a dope pusher. He was right. It was through Easy Money that Angel smoked her first joint. Of course, it wasn't long after she met Easy Money that she once again found herself pregnant.

Easy Money was excited. Although he had a dozen children already, he was excited because he felt that this baby was going to be cute…good hair you know…and maybe even hazel eyes.

He was right.

Just two days before her twenty-first birthday, Angel gave birth to a beautiful little girl she named Zee.

A month or so after Zee was born the police came to our house looking for Easy Money. They had a warrant for his arrest. He ended up going to prison because someone had set him up. (John confided in me many years after Easy Money had gone to prison that he was the one who told the police about Easy Money's "profession" and where he could be found. He said he wanted to help Angel do better for herself by getting rid of Easy Money.)

The years that followed brought a fairly decent man into Angel's life. His name was Aaron. He was in love with Angel and her children., Donte and Zee.

He encouraged Angel to move into an apartment with him. He took care of her and the children, and coerced her to take birth control pills so that she wouldn't get pregnant until they were ready.

Angel was happy. She loved Aaron more than she loved any other man she'd known.

Aaron encouraged her to put the children in daycare. Ever since she could remember, Angel had been taking care of my sisters and I, with only John to take care of her. Now, Aaron, a fine dark-chocolate colored brother, with muscles every place possible, was taking care of her. Life was too good!

Then, it happened. Hell broke loose…literally.

Easy Money was released from prison. He'd found out through some of his buddies on the street that Angel was living with Aaron. He was mad. Not only had "his woman" not bothered to visit him in jail, or except his collect calls, but she had his little girl shacking up with some other man! His ego couldn't handle this. So, he went to get his woman and his little girl back.

It was a sticky, hot summer Friday evening. Easy Money had been drinking and getting high. His mind began to wander back to Angel and how she had deserted him when he went to prison. After walking for hours, Easy Money found himself standing on the steps of Angel's apartment. He knocked on the door. As he stood there, fidgeting with the object in the right back pocket of his blue jeans, the door opened, with Aaron standing in front of it.

"Can I help you?" Aaron asked the stranger at his door.

"Yeah. Does Angel live here?" Easy Money blurted out, still fidgeting with his back pocket.

"Yeah. Who wants to know?"

"Easy. Easy Money. That's my name, and I'm her man. Didn't she tell you about me?"

Aaron stared at the trash on his doorstep for a moment. Then he slyly replied, "Easy Money…oh yeah…you're the one who's been in jail for the past four years. I've heard something about you…but not enough to matter."

"That's cute homeboy. Where's Angel? I came to get my woman and my baby girl, Zee."

"Man, you need to leave. Angel doesn't want to see you. And Zee…she's not a baby anymore…she's five-years-old.

Now leave before I call the police…" Aaron slammed the door in Easy Money's face.

Easy Money pounded on the door. "Angel," he yelled, loud enough for the neighbors to hear. "Come on baby. Big Daddy's here!"

Aaron opened the door and told Easy Money that the police were on the way. He then closed the door again.

Easy Money clicked. He took the gun out of his back right pocket and fired through the window of the door.

There was a scream…then a loud thump…a succession of screams…Angel's screams…the sound of sirens.

Easy Money ran, but he didn't get far before he was arrested. He was booked on a murder charge.

Yes…Easy Money killed Aaron. Angel was devastated.

At the age of twenty-seven, Angel met another man. His name was Eddy Joe, and he was married. He was a big man, both in height and in weight. He bought Angel a car and kept her rent paid. He even kept her supplied with the product he manufactured and sold: crack.

After about four months, Eddy Joe began to conduct business from Angel's apartment. One night, an associate of his made a pass at Angel. Eddy Joe blamed Angel because he said her shorts were too tight and too short. He said she looked like a hooker.

"Man, you are crazy! This is my apartment. My name is Angel, and I can dress any way I want to in my own house."

Angel saw it coming, but it was too late for her take back what she'd said. Eddy Joe got up from the green leather sofa. It took him a minute, because he was so big, it was hard to get up from the sofa, which kind of sunk in when he sat on it. He walked over to the kitchen door where Angel was standing with her left hand on her hip, and her right hand up to her mouth, which was clutching a cigarette. He never said a word, only smiled at her. With the speed of Muhammad Ali, Eddy Joe hit Angel so hard, he broke her jaw.

As she lay curled up on the floor, with her hand on her face, Eddy Joe looked down at her. He brushed his right hand over his head, and with his left hand, pointed at her. "Look here, girl, your name may be Angel, but my name is Eddy Joe. I don't allow *no* woman to talk back to me. You better recognize who I am and remember this night. If you ever disrespect me again, I will break your neck. Do you understand that?"

Angel didn't answer Eddy Joe. She was furious. He had broken her jaw, and probably messed up her face. She knew she needed Eddy Joe's financial help, and his drugs, but she was too feisty...had always been...to just let another man hit her. Her mind raced back to Aaron. He loved her. He had never hit her, or mistreated her. *He'd even died trying to protect her.*

Suddenly, she clicked. Just as Eddy Joe turned his back to her, Angel struck a match that lay next to her cigarettes that had fallen onto the floor from her shirt pocket when Eddy Joe hit her. She tossed the match towards Eddy Joe's shirt.

Fire...

Lots of fire...

Humph...

Eddy Joe on fire!

After a few minutes of wailing, Angel threw a blanket on Eddy Joe. She thought for a few minutes about whether she should let him continue to suffer or not. She finally called 911.

As she waited for the ambulance, Angel sat on the sofa, starring at Eddy Joe, who was in so much pain that he couldn't even speak.

When the ambulance took Eddy Joe to the hospital that night, Angel never saw, nor heard from him again. When the paramedics asked her how his clothes caught on fire, Angel said, very coldly, "He was playing with fire, and he got burnt."

Angel did find out that Eddy Joe's burns were third degree, and he was in the hospital for a long time.

Two years passed before Angel let another man get close to her or her children. The day of her thirtieth birthday, she threw herself a party.

"Look here little sister," I recall her saying to me. "Today, I am thirty-years-old. I have two kids, a raggedy apartment, and a raggedy car. The only man that really cared about me, besides John, is dead. And, I'm not doing anything with my life. But...today...I'm going to party! This is a celebration Deanna! A celebration of my screwed up life..." She sat on the porch with a beer in one hand, and a cigarette in the other.

I didn't know what to say. I felt sorry for her because her life was screwed up. But, the good thing was, she knew it. Therefore, she could do something to improve the situation she was in.

Angel met a guy that night at her party. He was thirty-five, appeared to be single, and an average looking guy. He wasn't all that, but that night he gave Angel what she needed: some attention.

Gary. That was his name. Gary Davidson. He was a mechanic at a local car dealership, and he was extremely attentive to Angel. And...at this point in her life, Gary was what she felt she needed.

He was funny. He had a charming personality, but most importantly, Angel said Gary had goals.

Gary helped Angel with her children and helped her get a job at a nursing home. Eventually, he moved in with her. Before long, Angel found out she was pregnant again.

Gary, who had no children, was elated.

About seven months into her pregnancy, a woman who said Gary was her husband confronted Angel. She told Angel that she and Gary had been married for ten years. She said they didn't have any children because she couldn't.

"Then, one day, about a year ago, Gary just left," Gary's wife told Angel, as the two stood on the sidewalk in front of Angel's apartment. "He called me a few days after that to tell me

44

that he needed some space...So, I let him have his space. But the other day, a friend of mine overheard him telling somebody that he was going to be a daddy. She knew that it wasn't me he was having a baby with, so I followed him from work a couple of times...and, here I am. Did he tell you he was married?" she asked, while puffing on a cigarette.

Angel was unprepared for this, but she didn't let it show. "No, he didn't tell me that he was married. But, then, I didn't ask him. I, for some reason, assumed he wasn't. I mean, in the beginning, Gary was always here. He'd go home when it got dark...he said he wanted to be a good example for my kids...Then after a couple of months, he asked me could he move in with me...to help me take care of my kids...I...I didn't know about you..." Angel could feel her face turning red.

After Gary's wife left, Angel began to have pains in her stomach.

"Donte...call Gary," she yelled to her son. "Tell him it's an emergency...I need to go to the hospital."

The baby, a two-pound curly-brown-haired boy arrived early. Gary asked Angel if they could name the baby Gary Jr. She agreed.

She'd fallen in love with Gary. So, she never mentioned the visit from his wife. And, Gary still lives with her, Donte, Zee, and Gary Jr.

I wonder how her life might have turned out if Helen, our mother had been there for her...

CHAPTER ELEVEN

JaLeesa

Quiet and reserved is JaLeesa's personality.

JaLeesa was John's favorite daughter because she looked like his mother.

Her life hasn't been as hectic as Angel's, but she's had her moments.

At the age of thirty, JaLeesa is married with two children, a boy and a girl. She works at a youth detention center, and her husband Andre is a production worker at a local distribution company. They live in a house not far from where we grew up.

JaLeesa didn't graduate from high school. She dropped out of school in the tenth grade because one of the teachers at the school called her stupid. JaLeesa had been taught by Angel, like the rest of us, not to let people insult her.

Angel, believe it or not, had been our "mother," and the things she taught us, stuck with us. Her teachings, no matter how immature some may have been, were basically what we had to pattern after.

Anyway, JaLessa cursed at the teacher, and was suspended from school. She never went back. She did, however, get her G.E.D.

When she turned sixteen, JaLeesa got a job at the corner store. It was the same store where Helen had left us. We'd kept in touch with the owner, who we saw at least once a week.

While working at the store, JaLeesa met a very interesting character whose name was Abdul.

Abdul was a twenty-year-old dark-skinned hustler. (As in hustling drugs for money.) Another thing he tried to hustle, was JaLeesa.

46

She hated Abdul. When she got to work each morning, Abdul was there. When she got off in the evening, Abdul was there, touching her hair…and trying to hold her hand.

"Ooh Baby. Let me take you to the movies," he'd say, with a sly smirk on his face.

"Abdul, leave me alone!" she'd say, with every ounce of hatred she could find within her small framed body.

One evening, while she was walking home from work, Abdul followed her. And by the time she made it to the front door, he was standing behind her. But she didn't know it. As she opened the front door, he pushed her inside and tried to force himself on her.

He was such a weakling. JaLeesa fought him like *she* was a man.

That day, Angel happened to be entertaining company. When she heard noises coming from the living room, she went to see what was going on.

She walked in the room to find JaLeesa beating the mess out of Abdul.

After that day, Abdul never showed up at JaLeesa's job again.

When JaLeesa turned eighteen, she met Andre, who was a delivery driver for the store.

At the age of twenty, Andre had a lot going for himself. He was cute, had a good paying job, and his own apartment. When he approached JaLeesa about going out on a date, she turned him down. In the back of her mind, she saw his efforts as a repeat of Abdul. But Roberto, the store's owner knew that Andre was sincere and encouraged JaLeesa to go out with him.

After almost two months, JaLeesa finally said yes to a date with Andre. She found out that he really was nice. They continued to date for almost two years.

On her twenty-first birthday, Andre asked JaLeesa to marry him. They were married five months later.

Andre wanted the best for JaLeesa. She'd confided in him about Helen and John's failed marriage, and he assured her that he'd do everything he could to make her happy. He even told her to quit her job at the store and enroll in some classes at the community college. JaLeesa was skeptical at first, but she was smart. And...she wanted to do better than Angel, who at that time wasn't doing very well.

After two years, JaLeesa obtained an Associates Degree in Mental Health. She felt as though she might be able to learn something about her family by taking classes that explained the mental, physical and social disorders of individuals.

Upon graduating, one of JaLeesa's professors, who'd been quite impressed with JaLeesa, helped her get a job at a center for youth who had behavior problems.

Andre felt as though they were making progress now. They both had good paying jobs. Therefore, he impressed upon JaLeesa the idea that they should have a baby.

JaLeesa was skeptical. She really didn't want to have any children. After the way Helen had abandoned us, JaLeesa felt that she wouldn't be a good mother. In her mind, the ability for a mother to abandon her babies might be hereditary. Furthermore, she knew what it felt like to be loved by a man, because John had loved us and taken care of us. She knew how to love Angel, Jazmine, and me because we were her sisters, and we'd experienced everything she'd experienced. But a baby, that was something she would have to love and care for...even if she and Andre ever separated.

JaLeesa had observed Angel, and she was determined not to make the same mistakes.

Andre didn't pressure JaLeesa about having a baby. Finally, after two years of indecisiveness, JaLeesa gave birth to twins, Andre Jr. and Andrea on her twenty-sixth birthday.

She was nervous the day she took the twins home. I was there that day when she suddenly began to cry. *Postpartum depression*, I thought to myself. I'd heard about it, but had never actually seen it in action. My big sister looked at me, as she sat on the blue sofa in her living room, and I shall never forget what she said to me.

"Deanna, the day Helen abandoned us at the store has always stuck with me. I cried myself to sleep every night until I was seven. I knew that John loved us, but I couldn't understand why Helen didn't. I thought maybe I'd done something to make her hate us. As a little girl, I thought it was my fault that the woman who I called "mother" didn't care about me.

"I didn't want to get pregnant. I tried everything I could to keep from getting pregnant. But God had other plans for me, Deanna. It was God's will that I get pregnant. It was God's will that I just so happened to get pregnant with twins.

"Deanna, when I saw my babies, just minutes after they were born, I knew that I loved them. There is no way I could ever abandon little Andre Jr. and Andrea. Helen damaged me as a child. But, having children of my own repaired an area of my heart that I didn't know could be repaired."

JaLeesa...she's a wonderful mother. And Andre...he's an excellent husband and father.

I'm happy for JaLeesa.

I'm proud of JaLeesa.

Most importantly, I'm glad she used our childhood, which was filled with stumbling blocks, and created stepping-stones to delegate the path her life would follow.

CHAPTER TWELVE

Deanna (*Me*)

I am the blessed one out of the bunch. Blessed because I had people to come into my life and encourage me to do more than just settle for the lesser things in life.

And, at the age of twenty-six, I can say that I am truly thankful for this blessing.

When I was in the sixth grade, I started a new school. On the first day, I met a teacher who became my inspiration.

She was so pretty, and kind. She even took the time to eat lunch with me several times a week. As a child, that meant a lot to me because I knew that she didn't have to make me feel important, but she did. She showed me what feeling special was like. By me being the third child, I didn't get much attention at home. So, I kind of indulged myself in TV and books.

Even though I made a lot of friends at school, what I looked forward to most of all was seeing Ms. Johnson each day. I remember one time when I was absent from school for a couple of days, Ms. Johnson went to the office and got my phone number and called me to see why I wasn't there.

I'd caught the pink eye from my nephew Donte. And, even though Angel had gotten some medicine for it, my eye just wasn't clearing up. The reason: everyone in the house was using the same bottle of eye drops, and continuously contaminating the infected areas. So, Ms. Johnson went to the school nurse and told her what was going on. A few hours after talking to me on the phone, Ms. Johnson and the school nurse showed up at my house with enough bottles of medicine for everyone to have their own.

After that school year, I went to another school, and lost contact with Ms. Johnson. I didn't adjust so well at this new school, and my grades were terrible. So, I started skipping school. Eventually, Angel realized that I wasn't going to school, but she didn't make me go.

As weeks turned into months, and months turned into years, I had been out of school for five years. I was sixteen-years-old. Yet still, I read a lot and watched educational programs on TV. I even helped Angel's children with their schoolwork.

One afternoon, while I was lying on the floor in the living room, watching TV, somebody knocked on the front door.

I opened it and found Ms. Johnson standing there. I couldn't believe my eyes. She had seen one of my sisters at the store and asked her how she could get in touch with me.

After a few days of lectures from Ms. Johnson about me not being in school, she enrolled me in a G.E.D. class.

Determined for me to obtain my G.E.D., Ms. Johnson transported me every morning to my class, and picked me up every evening. After only two months, I completed my course.

I could tell Ms. Johnson was proud of me. I was more proud of myself than she was.

Ms. Johnson encouraged me to apply for financial aid so that I could go to college. But, I decided to put it off for a little while. I needed some time to hang out with my boyfriend and party a little more.

One Friday evening in May, Ms. Johnson picked me up from my house and took me home with her. She talked to me and told me that I needed to figure out what it was that I wanted out of life. Did I want to be just another teenager with a baby? Did I want to be just another young mother living in a housing project? Did I want to be just another young woman that was to make up the statistics of struggling single mothers depending on the system to take care of me?

The answer to all of her questions was no. However, her lecture came a little bit too late. Just that week, I'd found out that I was pregnant. I didn't want to be, but I'd done nothing to prevent it.

She could tell by the expression on my face that I had something on my mind. She looked at me. Concern was in her eyes, and uncertainty in her face.

I recall the look on her face when I told her I was pregnant. She closed her eyes and managed to very quickly wipe away a tear that was rolling down her cheek.

I couldn't believe it, but that tear was for me. I couldn't recall anyone ever crying for me. Special. That's how she made me feel.

Ms. Johnson looked at me and said, "Deanna, you are a beautiful young woman. You have been through a lot in your short sixteen years. In a few months, you'll be seventeen. Do you think you are mature enough to be a mother?"

"I don't know. I wasn't trying to get pregnant."

"I know you weren't trying to get pregnant. But now, you have to realize that you are not only making decisions for yourself anymore. Everything you do now, will affect you…and your baby."

I remember crying. I also remember the last thing she said to me that day, as she dropped me off at home. She looked at me, and as tears began to overtake her eyes once again, Ms. Johnson said, "Deanna, you can't change what has happened. And you are getting more and more mature as each day goes by. Maturity is the art of living in peace with what we cannot change, the courage to change what should be changed and the wisdom to know the difference. Do the right thing, Deanna, for you and your baby."

All that night, I thought about what Ms. Johnson said to me.

I didn't want to be another single mother living on welfare, waiting each month for a check to come in the mail to be able to feed me, and my child.

I also knew that I didn't want my baby to grow up in the type of environment that was dangerous. I didn't want my child to refuse to strive for excellence. I didn't want to be looked upon as a sorry mother.

I cried a lot that night, and many nights after that. Finally, I got up the nerve to call Ms. Johnson. I told her that I had decided to go to college. I'd be able to finish a semester before the baby was born. I also told her I needed a job because I needed to get a decent apartment in a decent neighborhood. I was ready to be responsible for my actions and my child.

I could hear the sound of relief on the other end of the phone when I told Ms. Johnson of my plans. For a moment, she was silent. Eventually, she said she'd help me as best she could.

Two weeks later, I had a part-time job, my own apartment, and I was enrolled in the fall semester at the Jr. College.

Ms. Johnson paid my first and last months rent on an economy apartment; fully furnished in a nice, quiet neighborhood, close to the Jr. College. I lived close enough to walk.

John saw that I was trying to better myself, so he would come by in the mornings and drive me to school.

After a few weeks I met a young man, who seemed nice, in one of my classes. One day he saw me walking home and offered me a ride. My feet were so tired, and my back was aching, so I accepted his offer, praying all the way home that he wasn't a serial killer or something.

His name was David. He was kind of cute, and really smart. As he drove me home, he talked about the class and told me if I needed any help with the assignments, he'd be glad to help me. The class we were in together was College Algebra, and I was going to need all of the help I could get.

As we pulled up to my apartment, David asked me if I was married.

I told him no.

He asked me did I live alone.

I told him yes. Then, to deter any more questions, I told him that I was single and that I would be raising my baby alone.

To my surprise, David asked me for my phone number. For a moment, I hesitated. Then I wrote my number down on the corner of a piece of paper that had some notes on it, tore it off, and handed it to him. I didn't expect him to call me, but it was nice that although I was pregnant, four months at the time, and showing, someone still had the nerve to ask me for my number.

As I gathered my things to get out of the car, David quickly opened his driver's side door, and raced around to my side to open the door for me.

No one had ever opened a door for me. I almost didn't know how to react. But I remembered Ms. Johnson telling me that there were dogs in this world, and there were gentlemen in this world. She said that if it was anyway possible, try and keep company with a gentleman.

A gentleman…that's what David was. I smiled at him, as he helped me out of the car. He carried my books, like a schoolyard thing, as he walked me to my front door. As I unlocked the door, I turned to thank him for the ride.

He smiled at me and said, "No problem."

Later that afternoon, as I sat on the sofa, watching TV and eating a sandwich, my telephone rang.

"Hello," I answered, with food in my mouth. "Yes, this is Deanna." The voice on the other end of the phone belonged to David.

We talked on the phone for almost five hours that night. I finally told him I had to get off the phone because I had an eight o'clock class the next morning.

After hanging up, I realized how good it felt to talk to someone who cared about my thoughts and plans for the future. David had asked about the baby's father. I opened up to him and explained that I was trying to better my self; therefore, the baby's father was no longer in my life.

Before I went to sleep that night, I did two things. First, even though it was late, I called Ms. Johnson and told her about David. She sounded happy for me. The next thing I did was thank God for a glimpse of what it was like to be treated like a lady, and respected by a nice young man.

As the months passed, and December approached, David and I had gotten closer.

We studied for final exams together. I passed all of my classes and ended the semester with a 3.8 grade point average. I was really proud of myself.

One Saturday morning, about two weeks before Christmas, David showed up at my apartment with a Christmas tree. I was amazed at the size, as well as the beauty of it. I'd never had a real tree before. As a child, we always had artificial trees.

"Come on girl, show me where you want me to put this," he said, as he stood in the doorway, with the cold air slapping the back of his head. As he came in the door, I scanned the room for a moment, and decided to set the tree up in front of the window so passersby could behold it's beauty.

I'd been so busy with finals and the approaching arrival of the baby that I had forgotten about a Christmas tree.

"Deanna, get dressed so we can go shopping for some decorations," David said, as he put water in the pan under the tree.

"Okay, but give me a few minutes. You know I'm moving slower these days," I answered jokingly.

I remember shopping for lights, and ornaments. I remember being amazed by all the beautiful things I saw. My eyes danced, and my heart raced because this was the first time I'd actually be celebrating Christmas as an adult. I wouldn't be disappointed by not having a lot of gifts under the tree with my name on them. But this would be the Christmas that I would be giving myself more than anyone else could.

David picked up a couple of boxes of multicolored lights that played music when plugged in. I picked out some crystal ornaments that would glitter when the lights hit them. As we headed towards the check-out counter, my eyes fell on a beautiful African-American angel with rosy cheeks, happy eyes, crimson lips, flowing black hair, dressed in an ivory colored dress with gold trim. David saw the look on my face and reached for the box my eyes were fixed on. "We'll put her on top of the tree," he said with an angelic facial expression of his own.

Later on, after the tree was completely decorated, David and I sat on the floor. With the only lights on being those on the Christmas tree, and Christmas music playing, we enjoyed the beautiful sight before us.

I spent Christmas Eve of 1992 in the hospital. I was in labor. David was there, and so was Ms. Johnson.

As the clock struck 12:00 a.m., my son, Malik Anderson, was born. His birth was the best Christmas gift I could have received. It was even better than the ring David gave me that day, when he asked me to be his wife. I said yes, and in April of the following year we were married. He adopted Malik, and gave him his last name, Richardson.

Two years later, I graduated from the Jr. College. I then transferred to the local University to major in Education. David transferred as well, and majored in Engineering.

CHAPTER THIRTEEN

Jazmine

My baby sister's life was a little more complicated than the rest of ours. By her being "handicapped" she had to overcome a lot as a child and even more as an adult. Her obstacles didn't always have to do with the physical, but with the emotional.

She often thought back in time to when she was a baby, and the way our mother didn't love her. She blamed herself for the break up of our parents. Sometimes she pitied herself because of her handicap.

Our father had always treated Jazmine special, and so had we because we didn't want her to go through life feeling insecure.

By her being the baby, Jazmine learned a lot from the rest of us. She'd learned to walk early, she'd learned to talk early, she learned to read early, and even excelled in her schoolwork. She loved to read, and could always be found with a book in her possession.

Throughout elementary school, Jazmine had maintained a level of solitude as far as making friends. There was one little girl that she talked to named Carissa. Young children can be cruel, and Jazmine had been the target of many derogatory comments regarding her handicap. However, Carissa was the only little girl in school who hadn't made fun of Jazmine's hand. She, in fact, pretended not to notice. Therefore, the friendship between the two blossomed.

By the time Jazmine was in the seventh grade, she had become comfortable with herself. She'd learned to cope with her difference and didn't worry as much about trying to hide it from others. She and Carissa were still best friends and spent almost all of their time together.

By the time Jazmine was fifteen, she'd grown into a tall, beautiful shell, with a coke bottle shape. Boys were attracted to her looks, but she didn't give them a chance. She never worried about not having a boyfriend. She was concerned about maintaining her good grades, and not dropping out of school like the rest of us. She often talked about college and how she and Carissa would be roommates. She dreamed of becoming a lawyer.

During the beginning of her senior year in high school, Jazmine was approached by a school counselor named Rebecca Solis. Mrs. Solis had been looking through some of the students records, and noticed that Jazmine had excellent grades, and had earned enough credits to graduate early, with a 4.0 grade point average. She'd also located some scholarship opportunities for Jazmine and scheduled a time for them to meet so that they could fill out some scholarship applications.

Jazmine was elated. She couldn't wait to tell Carissa the news.

One rainy, Friday night in September, the two friends went to the movies to celebrate Jazmine's good fortune. As Carissa drove her mother's green Chevy Corsica home, a drunken driver lost control of his car and smashed into their car, causing the green Chevy Corsica to flip over. Carissa, who was not wearing a seat belt, was thrown from the car. She was killed instantly. Jazmine sustained a concussion, a broken arm, some cuts to her face from broken glass that required thirty stitches, as well as dozens of bruises.

At the scene of the accident, Jazmine had managed to crawl over to where Carissa lay lifeless on the wet grass on the side of the dark, slick rode. Paying no attention to her own pains, or the blood that was trickling down her face, she called out her friend's name, but her friend never responded. She tried to perform CPR on her friend, but to no avail. By the time help arrived, Jazmine, who had realized there was nothing that could be done for Carissa, was seated on the wet grass, with rain pouring down on her head, mascara running down her cheeks, cradling her dear friend in her arms. Tears were abundant, as her heart seemed to be breaking.

That night was a tragedy: not only because of Carissa's physical death, but also because of the emotional death of my baby sister.

Jazmine's whole attitude changed that night. I had to talk her into going to Carissa's funeral, which I do believe was the saddest thing I've ever seen in my life.

Jazmine missed a lot of school days after that. She told me that it was just too hard being there without Carissa. They'd shared the same locker, had almost all of their classes together, had eaten lunch together, and rode the bus home together.

About a month after Carissa's death, I asked Jazmine to talk to me because she'd become so withdrawn from everyone.

As she sat in a white plastic chair on the front porch, that breezy day in October, wearing the white t-shirt that had her picture with Carissa on the front, and monogrammed with the words, 'Carissa's Best Friend' on the back, her glassy stare was evidence that she was still in mourning. She puffed on a cigarette. Circles of gray smoke escaped her mouth. Smoking was a habit she'd acquired since the accident.

"Come on, Jazmine, I know you miss her. But…if you talk about her, maybe you'll feel better."

Jazmine never did glance my way. She continued puffing on her cigarette. After a few minutes, she managed to open her mouth. As a tear rolled down her cheek my baby sister uttered, "I can't believe she's dead. We were trying to decide which college we would attend. We'd even picked out our colors for our room we…we…would share…in the dorm…purple and turquoise. Purple was her favorite color; turquoise…mine. We were going to attend driver's education together this summer…but now, she's gone. Just like…" she ended her statement.

"Just like who Jazmine?"

"Like our moth— I mean Helen," she answered, almost whispering. A steady stream of tears rolled down her cheeks.

I leaned over to hug my baby sister. I couldn't stand to see her this way.

"No, baby sister. Carissa's nothing like Helen. You see, she didn't choose to leave you. God chose her. It was her time. But Helen…she chose to leave you…us. She made that decision on her own. She thought about nobody, but herself."

"Carissa would always tell me that beauty came from the inside. Then she'd tell me that I was a beautiful person inside and outside. She…never made me feel uncomfortable about my hand. In fact, at first, when I met her, I tried to act like it was nothing, and so did she. Eventually, she asked me about it. When she told me that my hand had nothing to do with my brain and that it had nothing to do with how I excelled in life…I knew she had a good heart…I knew she was beautiful too."

By November, Jazmine decided to take the opportunity given to her to graduate early. She found a job at a daycare center. She liked working with the babies. Somehow, she got in her mind that she wanted one…to love…the way Helen hadn't loved her. She knew that this wasn't part of the plans she'd made for herself, however she was still depressed about Carissa.

I don't believe any of us expected it when Jazmine began to display signs of being pregnant. She never told us whom she was pregnant by. However, she made it perfectly clear to everyone that she was keeping her baby and that she would take care of it.

In October of the following year, Jazmine gave birth to a beautiful, healthy little princess. She named her Bonita. It was the name Carissa had used in Spanish class, which meant *beautiful*.

Eventually, Jazmine tried to take classes at the Jr. College, but she kept quitting. She did however get a job working at an elementary school as a teacher's aide.

I wonder what Jazmine's life would have been like if Helen had been there for her. I wonder how Helen would have been able to comfort her youngest child who'd lost her best friend. I wonder how many of the plans Jazmine made for her future would she have actually fulfilled.

Although Jazmine is a wonderful mother, I believe my baby sister will always have emotional problems.

CHAPTER FOURTEEN

Helen

Over the years, Helen jumped from one relationship to another. She liked men who had money, and no children. She never talked about us, her children to the men she met. To her, it was easier pretending to be a single white female, than to explain to people about her ex-husband, who was black, and the four mixed daughters she grew tired of caring for.

Helen didn't keep a job. She was accustomed to men taking care of her, because John had done it. She was used to a man paying her bills, and buying her clothes and make-up because John had done it.

She'd begun to drink a lot after she abandoned us. She drank Vodka, Gin, Rum, Cognac, Crown Royal; anything containing alcohol. Many of the people she was acquainted with were alcoholics. So there was no chance that she'd stop.

After a while, the drinking and cigarette smoking began to take its toll on her body. She began to look bad. Even the expensive make-up and fancy clothes couldn't restore the beauty that was being destroyed by her nasty habits.

In 1990, she was diagnosed with diabetes. Her doctor told her she had to stop drinking and smoking. She told her doctor that she would try, knowing that as soon as she left his office, she'd light up another cancer stick and be on her way to the closest liquor store to get something to make her feel good.

Helen took her insulin shots like she was supposed to…only one shot a day, each morning. However, she continued to smoke between one to two packs of cigarettes a day.

In 1995, Helen met a mahogany colored man who resembled John a lot. His name was Will. He had a good job and was a kind-hearted person, just like John. He spoiled her and was eventually able to get her to cut down on her drinking. The smoking was a different story.

Helen and Will spent a lot of time together and eventually got married.

One day while Will was looking for something in the bedroom closet, he ran across a tan and black colored shoebox filled with dozens of pictures of little girls. Will took the tattered box out of the closet and set it on the bed. He continued to rummage through the box.

Helen came in the room and noticed it. She looked at the box for a long time. Then, she looked at Will.

"Helen," Will said in a calm, soothing voice, as he held a 5 x 7 photo in his hand. "Who are these beautiful little girls? They resemble you."

Helen's body language changed. She slowly walked towards the blue bedspread, which seemed to cradle the box of memories that she'd tucked away, deep in the closet. As she sat on the bed, it made a creaking sound. However, the noise didn't distract her because what was on her mind was what was in that box. The tan colored shoebox seemed to be pulling her like magnet. Eventually, she touched it. With the tip of her index finger on her right hand, she traced the rectangular shaped cardboard cage that held the spirit of her little girls, who now were adults, who had grown up without her guidance or protection. She thought of these little girls, whom she'd left at the corner store so many years before.

Tears began to fall from her eyes. She reached over to the nightstand and picked up her cigarette packet. She shook a single cigarette from the package, and then placed the pack back in its place. "Where's my lighter...I can't find my lighter," she said, as she looked around the room for it. She was trying to avoid eye contact with Will. He pulled a red cigarette lighter from the front pocket of his blue work shirt that displayed his name on a white patch. He walked over to his wife who was holding the cigarette in the corner of her mouth, between her crimson colored lips. With a flick of his thumb, a horizontal stream of fire appeared. Helen leaned forward to allow the cigarette to make contact with the fire. She took a long drawl. Then blew out a cloud of smoke. She crossed her legs, and as she held the cigarette between the tips of her fingers, looked up at her husband.

She made a motion by patting the bed, for Will to have a seat. She took another puff of her cigarette, and then began to talk at the same time the smoke was escaping from her mouth.

"Will, those are my girls." She took the picture he was still holding in his hand. "That's Jazmine, the day she came home from the hospital, and that's Angel, the oldest, JaLessa and Deanna."

"Why haven't you ever told me about them? Where are they?" he asked.

"It's a long story, but they live in Waco. They've lived there with their dad, my ex-husband since shortly after this picture was taken…almost seventeen years ago." She reached over to the ashtray on the nightstand to put her cigarette out. "I've never told you about them because…because I was ashamed."

"Ashamed of what?" he asked, while reaching over to hold her hand. "These are some beautiful girls."

She brushed his hand away, and then stood up to walk over to the window. As she stood there, looking at the puddles of water in the street, she sighed. "Ashamed…ashamed because…I abandoned them. That's what I did. I abandoned them…" She began to cough.

"What are you talking about Helen?"

Still coughing, she shook her head.

"I don't really want to talk about this anymore…" she left the room.

As she walked down the hall, to go to the kitchen, Will could still hear her coughing.

While she was getting a glass out of the cabinet, Will came in the kitchen and quickly went to the refrigerator to get the water pitcher. He walked over to Helen, who was leaning by the sink, still coughing. A look of terror came over his face as he poured water into her glass. Blood was on her hand.

"Baby, where's that blood coming from?" he asked, while reaching for a paper towel on the counter behind her.

She looked at her hand. And, as she coughed again...she realized that she was coughing up blood.

After about a week, Will was able to talk Helen into going to see her doctor.

He had bad news.

Helen had lung cancer.

CHAPTER FIFTEEN

A Moment of Silence

Sometimes, you just have a feeling that it's going to be a wild and crazy day. On that particular last Monday morning in November of 1997, I just couldn't see how things could get any better.

To begin with, my car wouldn't start. I was late for work at my job at a local elementary school. (I guess this would be a good time to mention that I finally finished college, and am now a teacher.) And of course, my husband and I had engaged in a disagreement about something that morning. I was in a funky mood.

On top of that, I'd received a notice the day before from the gas company. They were threatening to turn off my gas. It wasn't like we didn't have the money to pay the bill, we'd just been too busy. It had slipped my mind. The woman I spoke with on the phone in reference to making my payment was quite rude. She told me that I had to have my bill paid by 11:00 a.m. that morning, or I was going to be cold that night.

I'd tried to call Angel for a ride. She wasn't home. I'd tried to call Jazmine. She wasn't home either. So, I called JaLeesa.

"Hey, girl. I need you to come pick me up."

"Why?" JaLeesa asked. She sounded like she was brushing her teeth.

"Because my car won't start. I have to get to the utility office to pay my bill before they turn off my gas. And…I'm late for work. Now, come get me!"

"I'm on my way," she said and hung up the phone without saying good-bye.

Even if she were on her way, it would be at least thirty minutes before she reached my house because she lived on the other side of town. The distance wasn't really that great, but seeing as how every family has somebody slow in it, I mean really slow, JaLeesa was our family's little turtle.

Since I had a few minutes to kill, I decided to call John to see how he was doing. I hadn't spoken with him in a couple of days, which was unusual. He would normally take a few minutes out of each day to call each of his daughters and speak with each of his grandchildren.

I dialed his number. The line was busy. I pressed the redial button, but the line was still busy.

I noticed that there were crumbs on the brass and glass dinner table where David and Malik had eaten breakfast. I got a damp blue and beige plaid towel from the sink and wiped the table. Then, I grabbed the last piece of fried bacon from the blue plastic plate on the counter.

I pressed the redial button again. The line was still busy.

I browsed through the newspaper. I always enjoyed reading the comic strips, the advice column, my horoscope, and the classifieds, in that order.

I always skimmed through the little blocks in the classifieds. They always seemed to be so informative.

Finally, at 9:40 a.m., I heard JaLeesa's car pull into my driveway. Before she could blow her horn, I was already out the door.

As I got into her car, I teasingly said, "Dang, Girl, you have to be the slowest person in the world! What took you so long?" I was fastening my seatbelt when she looked at me in a kind of ticked off way.

"Just as I was walking out the door, some woman called trying to get me to change my long distance carrier," she said while backing out of my driveway.

As we drove down the street, I asked her had she heard from John. Just as she was about to answer me, I felt the car wobbling. I noticed she was pulling her car over to the side of the road. "What's up?" I asked.

"Didn't you feel that? Of all things, I gotta flat! Sh…"

"Do you know how to change a flat?" I asked her, as we both exited the gray Ford Escort.

"No, I don't know how to change a flat. So, I'm sure today's probably going to be a learning experience for the both of us."

By the time we figured out how to change the tire, I had less than fifteen minutes to get to the utility company. I'd called my job from a pay phone and was able to use car trouble as an excuse to not go to work at all.

I got my gas bill paid!

As soon as I got back home, my phone was ringing. It was a nurse at the hospital. She was calling to say that John had suffered a mild heart attack and that he'd asked her to call me.

Luckily, JaLeesa had decided to stay and visit for a while, so she was able to give me a ride to the hospital. We were both nervous.

When we arrived, John was asleep. A friendly nurse told us that he would be alright and would be able to go home in a couple of days.

JaLeesa and I were happy to hear good news.

Upon returning home later that evening, I noticed a strange phone number on my caller ID. I'm not one of those people who call strange numbers back, so I decided to erase it.

While preparing dinner, the phone rang again. Malik answered the phone, and within seconds was yelling my name.

After I dried my hands on a nearby towel, I looked on the caller ID in the kitchen. It was the same strange number I had deleted earlier.

"Hello," I said.

"Is this Deanna? Deanna Anderson?" A woman's voice said on the other end of the phone.

I'd begun to set the dinner table.

"Yes, this is she. Who's calling please?

"This is Virginia."

"Virginia...I'm sorry, I don't know anyone named Virginia."

"Virginia Davis-Stephenson. Your aunt...your mother's sister..." she answered. She seemed a little annoyed that I didn't know who she was.

"Oh...yes. Can I help you?" I'm sure I didn't sound very friendly. I hadn't seen nor heard from her in almost ten years.

"How are you?" she asked, with a nervous tone of voice.

"I'm okay..." I was wondering what she was calling me for. "And yourself?" I thought I'd be polite and ask.

"Well, that's why I'm calling. I'm afraid I have some bad news..." her voice started to crackle, as if she were trying to refrain from crying.

I found myself sitting at my place at the dinner table. I hadn't made a sound. My heart started to beat at a rather unusual pace.

"Deanna, are you there?"

"Yes...I'm still here."

I heard sadness in her voice as she said, "There's no easy way to say this...but...your mother has cancer. She's dying..." There was a moment of silence. Then she said, "She wants to see you...all of you." I heard her sniffle.

I was at a loss for words. My mind was racing. For a moment, my mind went to a memory I had of a woman waving good-bye from a car while my sisters and I were left alone...abandoned.

I must have been in a trance because I recall hearing her speak, but I couldn't speak back. Finally, I heard myself say, "Oh, I'm sorry to hear that. Could you hold for a second please?" I said. My phone was beeping, which was an indication that someone else was trying to call. I answered the other line. It was JaLeesa.

"Hey Sis. I was just calling to let you know..."

I interrupted her. "JaLeesa, guess who's on the other line...you'll never guess, so let me go ahead and tell you. It's Virginia."

"Virginia? Who's Virginia?" she asked.

"Helen's sister."

"Oh. What does she want?"

"Let me call you back, okay."

"Okay", she said. "I'll be waiting."

Once I'd clicked back over, Virginia quickly began a discussion. "I know this is sort of strange for you. But, she is dying. She has very little time left. She didn't ask me, but I told her I would see if I could get you girls to come visit her. She's in the hospital. Do you think you could…" her voice trailed off again.

There was another moment of silence.

I gathered my thoughts, then said, "Look, I haven't seen nor heard from Helen in over twenty years. I'm not sure if I care to see her now. What you want to ask me is if I can get my sisters to come see her. Well, I can't promise you that. I hope you didn't make any promises to her. I guess you were lucky that my phone number was listed in the phone book under my maiden name. Otherwise, you probably wouldn't have been able to call me with this news. I don't know how you expected for me to react to this news, or your request…but…I'll get back with you, okay. You have a good evening, Virginia." I said with a lot of anger in my voice as I hung up the phone.

I tried to compose myself. It was almost impossible to do.

My phone rang again. I thought it was my sister, so I said, "Yes JaLeesa, what can I do for you?"

I was embarrassed when Virginia said, "This isn't JaLeesa. I just called back to give you the name of the hospital and the room number, just in case you decide to go see her.

I listened to her ramble off the name of the hospital and the room number, but I didn't bother to write it down. After she was finished, I said goodbye to her for the second time.

I was still sitting at the kitchen table when my husband came in from the living room. I was in a daze, but I could hear him rattling pots.

"Baby, you're burning dinner. What's up?" he asked.

"Oh shoot...I forgot that I was cooking dinner." I said. I still hadn't moved from my seat. I'd developed a slight headache. David walked over and sat down beside me at the table. He placed his hand on my arm and with great concern in his voice said, "What's wrong? Who was that on the phone? Are you okay?"

I looked him in the eyes and said, "I'm not okay...that was bad news on the phone. Helen...my...mother is dying."

He looked at me surprisingly. Then reached over to hug me. As he held me in his arms, he said, "It's okay to cry honey."

Quickly, I moved away from my husband's affectionate arms. "I don't feel like crying. I just can't believe my aunt called me. Now, I've got to call my sisters." I got up and walked over to the sink. Then spoke softly, "Virginia wants us to go see her...before she dies."

"When are you going?" he asked, from behind me.

There was a moment of silence, as I thought to myself whether or not I would go. Part of me didn't want to. The other part of me felt...numb.

A few hours later, after I'd cleaned up the kitchen and gotten Malik to bed, I called JaLeesa and Angel on three-way and told them what Virginia said.

For almost thirty seconds, I couldn't hear any breathing on the phone. It was completely silent. I knew what they were thinking. I knew what they were feeling.

"Well, what do you want to do?" I asked them, hoping they would have a solution to our problem.

Angel spoke first. "I don't want to see her. I think I'd just prefer to remember her smiling and laughing. And, that day she abandoned us at the store, she seemed pretty damn happy to me."

Then JaLeesa spoke. "I hear what you're saying Angel. But maybe she wants to apologize to us. Maybe she..."

Angel cut off JaLeesa's comment. "I don't think an apology is going to take away any of the feelings we've carried with us for over twenty years. I don't think the words *I'm sorry* will make up for the lack of a childhood I had because I was the oldest, and was therefore responsible for everybody else. I don't think the words *I'm sorry* will make me change the way I feel about her. Now that she's dying, she wants to see us. Well, what about all of the birthdays we've had? She didn't call us. What about all of the Christmases we have had? She never brought us presents or even called to say hello. John was the one who took care of us." Angel was quiet for a moment, and then she asked me, "Have you told Jazmine. You know that her life has been more affected by Helen than the rest of ours."

"No, I haven't told her yet. This is complicated for us because we knew that she was leaving us. For Jazmine, it's a different kind of complication because she knows that after she was born everything for Helen and John changed for the worse, and she has always felt that she was the blame. You know she has always wondered why Helen didn't love her."

"Well, I don't think you should tell Jazmine over the phone," JaLeesa said. "I think we should meet at her house tomorrow, and discuss this situation together; face to face.

"Okay...it's getting pretty late. I'll see you tomorrow." I said, and hung up the phone.

I didn't sleep that night. I had too much anger in my heart. Although my husband slept with his arm around me, I still felt lonely.

The next day, my sisters and I missed work. We met at Jazmine's house, like we'd agreed.

As we talked, I noticed that none of us shed tears. We were all remembering the biggest factor in our relationship with Helen...the fact that she'd abandoned us.

After a while, we decided that we didn't want to see her, sick and dying. What we'd always wanted...we'd never gotten...*a mother.*

On Thursday of that week, Virginia called again. But this time, I didn't answer the phone. I looked at the caller ID, and just let the phone keep ringing. I didn't want to hear anything else about Helen.

By the weekend, my husband had decided that he'd had enough of my unpleasantness.

I remember that Saturday morning; he brought me breakfast in bed. I remember he'd lit candles all over the bedroom, to help relieve my stress. I hadn't realized how that phone call from Virginia had affected me.

"Deanna, I want you to listen to me for a minute. Don't speak…just listen. I've watched you this week, and I don't think you made the decision you wanted to make. I think you really want to go see Helen, but you feel like you have something to prove by not going. Today, I want you to get dressed, and we'll go to the hospital, together. I'll get my sister to watch Malik. Maybe it won't be as bad as you think. You've got to let go of this anger you have for her. It's eating you up."

"Maybe you're right…I'll go. But don't tell my sisters. I feel like I'm betraying them," I told him as I slipped out of bed and got dressed.

The drive to the hospital seemed to take forever. The fact that the men on the radio were singing, "*it was just my imagination, running away with me…*" didn't make the situation any better. When we got to the hospital, the corridors seemed to go on forever.

When we finally got to the floor where Helen was, I started feeling dizzy.

"David, I need to sit down for a minute," I said while heading to a bench in the lobby.

"Baby, I know this isn't easy for you. But, it might make you feel better…about her. Just knowing that you've done the right thing will make you feel better in the long run."

I finally got up the energy to continue my journey. I found myself standing in front of her room.

As I stood in front of the door, my legs froze. David opened the door for me. When we peeked inside the room, it was empty. My husband and I looked at each other.

David turned to find a nurse, while I continued to stand there, still frozen.

As he walked towards me, I could tell by the look on his face that something was wrong.

Helen had passed away at three o'clock that morning.

David put his arms around me.

I didn't cry, nor did I feel like crying, but I was glad he was there with me.

CHAPTER SIXTEEN

Flashback

I've already told you about Helen's funeral. However, I didn't tell you about how Helen's husband approached us at Virginia's house.

My sisters and I, who were standing in a corner talking amongst ourselves, were feeling out of place. We hadn't been around any of these people, our *family*, since we were children. It was John who insisted that we accept Virginia's offer to join her for dinner at her house after the graveside services.

We noticed a mahogany colored man in a black trench coat watching us. Angel was beginning to get annoyed.

Finally, the tall, mahogany colored man walked over to us. He pulled up a chair and sat down.

"I know that you are wondering who I am, and since no one has bothered to introduce us, I'll take it upon myself to do the honors. I'm Will, your mother's husband. I hope you ladies don't mind me interrupting you, but I just felt that I should give you a message your mother asked me to deliver, just in case I ever had the privilege to meet you." Will crossed his legs, and placed his hands over his knees. Then, he continued, "Your mother asked me to tell you that she was sorry and that she understood why you didn't come see her when she was sick…"

Angel interrupted Will's speech.

"Listen, Will, it's really nice of you to tell us what our mother said to you. But, you're not the one who should be telling us what *she* said. Helen should have told us this a long time ago. She's had plenty of time to tell us she was sorry. So, coming from you, doesn't make us feel any better." She was working her neck and pointing her finger in a very attitudinal manner.

Will held his composure. "Okay, I understand this is probably not the right time or place for this conversation. But, if you ladies ever have any questions about your mother, feel free to call me." He got up from the chair, placed it back where he'd gotten it from, then walked over to Virginia. He hugged her softly, and walked out the front door.

CHAPTER SEVENTEEN

Closure

Five months after Helen's death, I was finally able to cry. I don't really know how it happened, but once I started, I could not stop. I'd recently given birth to my second child, a daughter, who I named Chyil. Therefore, I was home on maternity leave.

I can remember watching a talk show on television. The topic for the day was *Dealing With Your Past.*

One of the guests on the show talked about her relationship with her mother, and how bad it was. She said that when her mother died, she felt no emotion. However, now she was severely depressed.

A psychiatrist on the show said that she needed to get in touch with her emotions. She told her that it was not good to keep her true feelings bottled up inside.

"What you need to do," I recall the lady saying to the guest, "is…write a letter to your mother. Even though she is no longer physically present…she is emotionally and mentally a part of your life. You need to write her a letter to express what you are feeling inside. Then, seal the letter in an envelope. And…if it will make you feel better, flush it down the toilet and watch your emotional baggage go down the drain…"

It *sounded* like a good idea, but I had no idea where to begin.

I remember getting up from the sofa. I walked over to the drawer in the kitchen where I kept a notepad and pens.

I recall taking a deep breath as I walked over to the kitchen table, pulled out a chair and sat down.

"Dear Lord, guide me," I prayed, as I found a page in the note pad that didn't have crayon or scribble marks on it.

I sat there for a moment trying to figure out where to begin. Through the window, I could see Malik playing in the dirt in the front yard, while Chyil was sleeping in her crib in her room. I was determined not to allow the rowdiness of the neighborhood

77

children outside to distract me, as I tried to concentrate. My mind kept wandering.

Eventually, yet slowly, thoughts began to flow, and so did the tears that I'd held back for almost all of my life.

I began to write…a letter to Helen…my mother.

"Dear Mother,

It has been five months since we buried you. Five months since you disappeared for the last time. Five months since you went away for another long break…from us, your children.

Your departure from our lives five months ago was unexpected. But the sad part about it is that I was all cried out. My tears for you would no longer fall.

Even at your graveside service, I felt no emotion for you. I really started not to go. But, I just couldn't miss your final exit from my life. I feel more comfortable at this moment referring to you as Helen. Although you gave me life, you were never there to help me live it. You were never there to encourage me, or hold me, or teach me about life. You were never there to protect me. You were never there, to be my mother. All of us, your children, were really motherless children because you never did take responsibility for us. You never nurtured us, or loved us.

I feel as though we were all a product of your misguidance on birth control prevention.

You have no idea how many nights as a child I cried because you made me feel as though I had done something wrong.

Eventually, Helen, I will get over the pain I have felt because of your lack of "mothering". I often wondered what I did, or what any of us did, to make you not want to love me. I wondered how a mother could drive away, and not turn back, knowing that she wouldn't come back, while her little girls stood frightened and alone on the steps of a convenience store.

God has been good to me, Helen. It is because of Him, that I can write you this letter. I'm crying now. But these tears I shed are for you. These tears I shed are for you because I feel sorry for you. I feel sorry for you because you never got to know what it was like to watch your children grow. You never got the chance to feel the love that children represent and share.

My heart goes out to you. Even though you never gave me a chance to have a normal life, or to experience normal things, I learned something from you.

From you, I learned the importance of loving and caring for my children. I learned the importance of raising my children, and the necessity of stability in my children's lives. Due to your motherless characteristics, I am determined to be a good mother. I am encouraged by your lack of motherly commitment to never put my children in danger or have them feel that I don't love them, or that I don't care about them.

Because of you, I know the importance of seeing my children each morning, and tucking them in to bed at night. I know the importance of wiping away tears, and hugging away aches and pains. I know what it's like to stay up all night with a child who has a high fever. I know how big a difference a band-aid can make to a child. I know that I'm responsible for washing my children's clothes, and bathing my children. I know that I'm supposed to cook dinner, and still have time to read a bedtime story. But most importantly, I know when my little boy tells me that he loves me; all the sacrifices I've made for him are worth it.

Thank you, Helen. Thank you for setting an example for me not to follow. Thank you for giving me life. Thank you for showing me what it feels like not to be loved.

May God bless you, wherever you are.

Your Daughter - Deanna

Upon finishing my letter, I sealed it in an envelope. On the front of the envelope, I wrote Helen's name. I then placed the sealed envelope in my Bible that was on the shelf behind me.

Over the next two weeks, I began to feel better. My spirits had been lifted. I guess there really was a need to get my feelings out in the open. Writing the letter helped me to be able to cry again. It helped me to release those emotions that I'd had inside of me ever since…ever since I was a little girl.

It took me four months to flush the letter down the toilet. But the day that I did flush it, I fell down on my knees and thanked God for giving me the strength to overcome all of the obstacles and stumbling blocks that had been thrown in my path. However, I was still angry with Helen.

A short while after that, my selective memory allowed me the opportunity to recall some of the words to a song I'd heard once while playing in the front yard of our home when I was a little girl. An elderly black woman was often heard singing while she sat in a rocking chair on her front porch. Once, she sang a song about the Motherless Children.

In a deep alto voice, the old woman would sing: "*Motherless children have a hard time when their mother is gone…Motherless children have a hard time when their mother is gone…Father will do the **best he can**…Dear old fathers just don't understand…That's why motherless children have a hard time when their mother is gone…*"

That song was about my sisters and me. We were the motherless children she spoke of in her song. I'd never heard that song before, and I haven't heard it since.

As I took the time to look back over my life, and looked at where I came from, and the direction in which I was headed, I knew that I was truly a blessed individual.

CHAPTER EIGHTEEN

Something Unexpected

One Tuesday morning, about a year after Helen died, I was reading the classified section of the newspaper. I was looking for a new sofa, but hated to pay the price of a new one.

As I allowed my fingers to lead my eyes down the columns in the classifieds, that cold, rainy morning, November 3, 1998, I swear my heart stopped beating for a moment, as I felt the need to reread what I'd already read.

The ad said: Looking for Helen E. Davis, born June 1950 in Brownwood, TX, or anyone who knows her. There was a long distance phone number and additional words that instructed me to leave a message.

I wondered who could be looking for relatives of Helen. I also wondered why if they knew so much pertinent information, such as her name, date of birth, and place of birth, why they didn't know where to find Virginia.

I looked at my watch. It was time to go to work. So, I left the newspaper on the counter, and walked out the door.

All day, I thought about the ad in the paper. I wondered if anyone else had seen it. I wondered if I should call the number listed.

That evening, as I walked into the kitchen, the newspaper ad seemed to be taunting me. I walked over to it. I allowed my finger to trace the box that contained Helen's name. Then, without thought, I picked up the receiver of the phone and dialed the number in the paper. The phone started to ring. After the first ring, I placed the receiver back on its base.

I didn't know what I was nervous about. I dialed the number again. This time, I dared myself to let the phone ring until someone answered it. My heart stopped when a woman's voice said, "Hello…" There was a pause. Then, again, the voice said,

"Hello, I'm sorry I'm not available to take your call at this moment. Please leave a message, and I'll call you back. Thank you, and have a blessed day." Then there was a beep.

I'd gotten the answering machine. Well, I stammered for a moment, then found the words to say. "Hello...I'm calling about your ad in the newspaper. My name is Deanna, and you can reach me at..."

After hanging up the phone, I felt a little leery. Maybe I shouldn't have done that. But by then, it was too late.

It was almost a week after I'd left that message for the ad in the paper that I got a phone call. The caller ID didn't show a number. I assumed it was a telemarketer trying to sell me something.

I'd been watching a movie on Lifetime, the *women's channel*, as my husband referred to it. It was another one of those tearjerkers where the woman finds the courage to leave an abusive relationship, and in the process, finds true love. So, in an effort to quickly get back to my movie, I yanked the phone off the base.

"Hello," I said, trying to sound annoyed.

"Hello. May I speak with Deanna please?" a female voice asked politely.

"This is Deanna."

"Deanna, my name is Cecillya. You answered an ad I placed in the newspaper."

I sat up on the sofa and pressed the mute button on the remote control.

"Uh-huh," was all I could say.

"Well, as you already know, I'm trying to locate Helen Davis, or anyone who knows her. Do you know where I can find her?"

"I'm sorry...I guess I should ask why you're looking for her? You've told me your name, but who are you?"

"Well...on November 10,1967, Helen gave birth to a little girl. I'm that little girl. Well, I'm an adult now. I was given up for adoption. I'm thirty-one years old now, and I'd like to find her, and any relatives I may have. My adoptive parents were killed two years ago in a car accident.

I found some papers while I was going through some boxes in their bedroom. One paper was a birth certificate, which had Helen's name on it as the mother, and the other papers were official adoption papers."

I was at a loss for words. No one had ever mentioned anything to us about Helen giving a baby up for adoption.

"Well, Helen was my mother," I said. "But…she died last year. I'm twenty-five-years-old. I have three other sisters, Angel, JaLeesa and Jazmine…"

We talked for two hours and thirty-seven minutes that night. After hanging up the phone, I called John.

He confirmed that Helen had been forced to give their first-born baby girl up for adoption by her father in 1967. He seemed relieved to know that the child they'd created was alive and doing well.

I felt inclined, after hearing John's story, to call Cecillya back that same night. We made plans for her to meet the family in person.

Even though the hour hand and the minute hand were both sitting on twelve, a.m. that is, I still had three more phone calls to make. I started with Angel, but told each of my sisters the same thing.

"Hi, Sis. I know it's late, but I just thought you'd like to know that we have another sister. Her name is Cecillya, and she was given up for adoption by Helen in…"

CHAPTER NINETEEN

Cecillya's Lesson

It was cold that Saturday morning, the second week of November.

I was the first to meet Cecillya in person. I'd given her directions to my home because I was anxious to see what she was like.

Cecillya was a beautiful, young-looking woman, who was kind of beige in color. As I stared at her, I could see a little of each one of us, John, Helen, Angel, JaLeesa, Jazmine, and myself, in her.

She'd been raised by a black Baptist preacher and his wife, and had no idea until after their death that she was half white. She'd graduated from an all black college, and was the owner of a chain of childcare centers. She was married to a minister, and was the proud mother of two daughters.

I could see the difference having a mother and a stable household had made in Cecillya's life. She was everything I wished I could be…poised, confident, cheery, starry-eyed, with a figure to die for…all that, and more. These traits I'm sure she gained by the type of home she was fortunate to have been raised in.

We talked for hours, comparing stories of our childhoods. When she asked me what Helen was like, I hesitated, and then said, "To be honest, Cecillya, you and I have several things in common when it comes to Helen. I don't really know what Helen was like because she didn't raise my sisters and me. She gave you up for adoption when you were born because her father made her. She also gave us up, but then it was her own choice. She gave Jazmine to John shortly after she was born because she was born with a slight handicap. Then…when Angel was seven, JaLeesa was six, and I was two, she dropped us off at a neighborhood store, and…drove off. She abandoned us…"

CaSaundra W. Foreman-Harris

There was a look of disbelief in Cecillya's face. After listening to me for a while, she said, "Well, little sister...that sounds funny, but I've always wanted to be able to call someone that...you know I come from a religious family, and I know that you'll probably think I'm crazy when I say this. You've got to forgive Helen for what she did to you. I'm not going to preach to you, Deanna, but the Bible teaches us that we have to forgive those who trespass against us. It wouldn't be right if I didn't tell you this, but you've got to find a way to let go...you've got to let God show you how to forgive Helen for not being there for you. All of us must find a way to forgive Helen."

I looked at Cecillya, trying to figure out what she needed to forgive Helen for. She must have read my mind.

As she slipped off her heels, and made herself comfortable on the sofa, she nodded her head, and said, "Yes...even me. When I first found out that I was adopted, I was angry. I was angry with my parents for not telling me...and angry with whomever this Helen woman was because she didn't keep me. But...I had to pray about my situation. God reminded me that everything happens to us for a reason. Just like there's a reason that *you and I* are here, right now, together. Just like there's a reason *you* ran across my ad in the newspaper. Girl, I've been running that ad for a year. No one has ever answered it.

"So, I want you to think about this: maybe things happened in your life the way they did to teach you how to be a better mother than Helen was. You've learned from experience how important a mother is to a child."

I had begun to cry. The words she spoke purged my heart. She took a tissue from her purse, and wiped the tears from my eyes, with gentleness and loving-kindness. It was just the way I remember Ms. Johnson, my teacher and mentor, had done it so many years ago.

"Deanna, I would like for you to go with me to visit Helen's grave. I believe that if we go together, and pray together at her grave, our burdens will be released, and all those angry feelings you need to get rid of...God will rid you of them."

86

We did go visit Helen's grave.

As I stood at Helen's gravesite, which I hadn't visited in almost a year, feeling the cold air on my face, I closed my eyes and said my silent prayer while Cecillya said a silent prayer of her own.

It only took a few minutes, but Cecillya was right. After twenty-three years, prayer was what it took for me to finally be able to forgive Helen for the emotional pain she'd caused in my life.

CHAPTER TWENTY

The Power of Words

Eventually that afternoon, after Cecillya and I had gone to visit Helen's grave, she met the rest of the family who'd gathered at JaLeesa's house.

As Cecillya and I, along with Chyil and Malik, walked up to the front door of JaLeesa's red brick one-story home, John opened it. He had a huge grin on his face as he stood there, staring at Cecillya.

I took Chyil from Cecillya so that she could greet John, as he stood in the doorway in his khaki slacks and blue polo-style shirt with his arms positioned for a hug.

I remember seeing a tear roll down his cheek as his eldest daughter embraced him.

Cecillya smiled as she said, "You must be John. I'm glad to meet you."

John was so choked up that he could not speak. I wondered what he was feeling at that moment…I wondered what he was thinking at that moment. Whatever was on John's mind at that moment, was interrupted by my sisters who were standing behind him in the living room. Before John released his embrace with Cecillya, he uttered, in almost a whisper, "You…you are so beautiful. I've often wondered what you looked like, and whether or not you were okay…"

After hugging everyone in the house, Cecillya made herself comfortable on the floor. Sitting on the floor…something Jazmine and I both enjoyed doing, as did John.

We talked, looked at old photos, looked at recent photos, laughed a lot…and cried a little.

We found out just how much we were all alike by the birthmark each us had on our left shoulder. It was a little brown circle. I always thought it was the ugliest thing on my body.

That day, I found out that all of my sisters felt the same way about their little brown circle.

John had gone outside for a cigarette. Upon reentering the room, he cleared his throat. Everyone stopped talking and looked at him.

"Well ladies," he said, as he made himself comfortable on the sofa beside Jazmine. "I must say that this is one of the happiest moments of my life. To see all of my girls...excuse me...my daughters...here, together. It just makes my heart full of joy.

"I know that you ladies have had a hard time growing up...with the exception of you Cecillya." He paused for a moment, as he looked at his eldest daughter. He scratched his head, then said, "Cecillya—when Helen found out that she was pregnant with you, we were going to make plans to be together. But...her daddy...he didn't like black people...and he decided that he would send Helen away so she could have the baby, and give it, I mean you, up for adoption. Helen was heartbroken for a long time after you were born. She secretly named you Faith. I'm glad you have been fortunate to have done well in life. I still can't believe that you are here." He wasn't finished. He seemed to have a lot on his mind. He looked around the room, as he took a sip of the beer he held in his hand.

"I want the rest of you girls to know, especially you Jazmine, that you shouldn't be angry with Helen anymore for abandoning you. She was a good mother and a good wife...you girls know that I have always loved her. She just...I don't know...I guess she just got tired. Everything happened too quickly...becoming a mother...a wife...and, times were tough back then. We didn't have a lot of money. We had just enough to make ends meet.

"I've never told you this, but that day...that day she abandoned you at the store...I was at work. I got this phone call. There was some man on the phone telling me that he had my three little girls in his store. I told him he must have the wrong person, because my three little girls didn't live in Waco. Then I heard him ask Angel what was her name. And…when I heard her voice…my heart almost dropped to the floor.

"That man only knew me because I bought cigarettes and beer in his store, and sometimes I paid by check. It must have been one of God's Angels watching out for us, because that crazy man hadn't made a deposit in three days. And that's how he found me…he called my work number he'd written on the back of my check." He laughed.

As I looked around the room, I saw something amazing. A man…our father…who had the utmost respect of his daughters, had managed to make them teary-eyed. We'd never heard John talk like this before. He'd always kept things…his thoughts to himself.

Angel was the first to speak, and what she said were the most powerful words she'd ever spoken.

"Daddy…I want you to know that I appreciate you being my dad. I know that there are a lot of men out there who don't take care of their children. I know that there are a lot men out there who would have tried to put their daughters off on someone else. But you…you've loved us and taken care of us since the day we were born. I remember watching you change diapers and wash dishes. I remember watching you cook and clean. I remember you rocking my sisters to sleep at night and waking us in the morning. I remember you making me…all of us…feel loved.

"And, I know that I haven't always made the best choices, but you've never downed me. And…I want you to know that I appreciate you, and love you. I'm sorry for putting you through hell in my ***wanting to be grown years***. But…I'm glad you are my dad."

By the time Angel finished talking, John could no longer keep his composure. He broke down.

Jazmine reached over and held his hand.

That was the first time I'd ever seen my father cry.

It was getting late, and Cecillya was going to drive back home the next morning. As she began to gather her things to head back to my house, where she was going to spend the night, she suddenly exclaimed, "I forgot to do two things."

Cecillya reached inside her purse and pulled out a camera. "Someone is going to have to take our picture."

JaLeesa's husband volunteered.

Afterwards, Cecillya reached inside her gigantic purse again and pulled out a letter-sized white envelope.

"Okay ladies...my sisters...my little sisters...I know that we will be seeing each other again soon. But, I wanted to share something with you that really has helped me get through some tough times in my life." Cecillya opened the envelope and handed each of us a lilac colored bookmarker with gold writing. "Now, I know you are probably saying, "Why is she giving us a book marker...well...the words on the bookmarker are powerful. You don't have to read it now. When you get home...and have a few moments to yourselves...read the words that make this bookmarker special."

Cecillya drove back to Oklahoma the next morning. As I'd watched her back out of my driveway in her mini van at 4:00 a.m. that cold, drizzling, Sunday morning in November, I felt so...happy inside.

I would have never thought that I could feel...peace the way I was feeling at that moment.

As I went to climb back in my bed, I remember the lilac bookmarker Cecillya had given each of us.

I climbed back out of bed, trying not to disturb my husband and went into the living room where I'd placed the bookmarker inside my Bible, for safekeeping.

As I turned on the lamp beside my desk that harbored my Bible, I sat down on the chair that my husband called his *thinking chair*. I held the lilac bookmarker up to the light so that I could see.

On one side of the bookmarker, were the words: ***To my sister Deanna. May God Bless You. Love, Cecillya.***

On the other side of the bookmarker was this:

WHAT MATTERS
BY SERENITY WILSON

It doesn't matter where I came from-
What matters is where I'm going.
It doesn't matter how little I've had-
What matters is how much I appreciate what I have.
It doesn't matter who has more than me-
What matters is how I use what I have to be a blessing to
   someone else.
It doesn't matter who hurt me-
What matters is that I forgive them.
It doesn't matter how angry I was yesterday-
What matters is that today is a new day.
It doesn't matter what they say-
What matters is what I know.
I doesn't matter how I look-
What matters is how I love.
It doesn't matter how important I think I am-
What matters is how important I make others feel.
It doesn't matter how smart I think I am-
What matters is that I don't belittle someone else.
It doesn't matter how many road blocks have been
   placed in my path-
What matters is how I use my wit to get around them.
It doesn't matter how I feel about myself-
If I don't matter to God.

CHAPTER TWENTY-ONE

Saying Goodbye

At 10:30 am that same Sunday morning, I was rushing my husband. He was moving so slowly and I hated to be late for church.

The phone rang. I thought to myself, *I don't have time to talk on the phone right now.* So, I looked on the Caller ID. It was JaLeesa.

"Hello," I said, while trying to get Chyil's hair ribbon tied.

"Deanna," JaLeesa said. I could hear sadness in her voice. She was crying.

"What's wrong?" I asked her.

"Deanna, I've got some sad news. I went in to wake up John this morning, and he wouldn't wake up. Deanna, he died in his sleep..."

I couldn't believe what I was hearing.

"What?" I exclaimed, as I put Chyil in her playpen. I stood up to go into my bedroom, where David was. I didn't want Chyil or Malik to see me cry. "Are you sure?"

"Yes. I called 911 and they came. They took him to the hospital, where they pronounced him dead. But...he actually died at home."

"Can you come over? We need to make funeral arrangements," JaLeesa said. She was crying harder than she was when she first called.

"I'll be there as quickly as I can. Have you called Angel or Jazmine?"

"No...you know I always call you first. I'll call them now."

I hung up the phone. For a few minutes, I sat there on the corner of my bed, frozen.

David was ready to go now and was looking at himself in the mirror. He was such a handsome man, and a wonderful husband and father.

"I'm ready…let's go," he said.

As David turned around, he noticed that I was crying. "Baby…" he said, "What's wrong?" He sat down beside me on the bed. He took the handkerchief out of his pants pocket and wiped my face where tears of sadness marked their territory.

"He's gone David…" was all I could say.

"Who's gone?" he asked, looking confused.

"John…My father. That was JaLeesa on the phone. She said that John died in his sleep this morning…" At that point, I broke down and cried harder than I'd ever cried before in my life. My husband pulled me close to him, and tried to take away the pain I was feeling.

"I just can't believe it. Last night he was talking to us…saying how happy he was. And now, he's gone."

I could feel David's heart beat, as he took a deep breath. "Deanna, yesterday was probably one of the proudest moments of your dad's life. He had all of his children and almost all of his grandchildren in one place. When I went into JaLeesa's kitchen last night to get a drink, I heard the stuff you and your sisters were saying to him, and the things he was saying to you and your sisters. He seemed relieved last night. Do you remember when he got up to go to the restroom? I passed him in the hallway. Do you know what he said to me?"

I shook my head, signifying no.

"He said, "David, I'm okay now. I know my girl's love me and they know I love them. They are all happy, and they are all doing well. For a long time, I worried about them because of what their mother did to them. But now, I can…breath. My soul can rest now. My soul can rest…""

"I wasn't sure what he meant by that, but now I know."

I looked at David. I could see what he was getting at.

Four days later, my sisters and I were once again dressed in black and at another gravesite.

John had always said that he didn't wan't a long, drawn out funeral. He'd always said, "a graveside service is good enough. That way, you don't have to spend a lot of money. "Cause funeral homes get over on dead folks families."

So, there we stood; Cecillya, Angel, JaLeesa, Jazmine and me, with our families and John's sisters and friends.

This time, unlike the funeral we'd attended less than a year before for Helen, there was crying...lot's of crying. We were saying goodbye to the man, our father, who'd helped bring us into this world, and took care of us until the day he died.

John's casket was surrounded by people who truly loved and adored him.

John's casket was surrounded by people who respected and admired him. His death was unexpected and greatly affected each of us.

We hardly noticed the cold drops of rain that had begun to fall from the sky. Those drops were minute compared to our tears...tears we were shedding for John...our dad.

Two weeks after we buried John, I received a letter in the mail from John's insurance company. The letter explained that John had named me as the beneficiary of his life insurance policy. John had left instructions for me to divide the enclosed check amongst my sisters and myself. As I turned over the check enclosed with the letter, I almost fainted. The insurance check in my name was in the amount of one-hundred thousand dollars. I immediately begin to cry. John was still taking care of his girls, just the way he had always done.

Although my sisters and I were thankful for the monetary blessing of twenty-thousand dollars each, we were more thankful that we'd been blessed to have a man like John for our father.

My name is Deanna, and this is my story; the story of *The Motherless Children.*

The Beauty…Within
By CaSaundra W. Foreman-Harris

I caught a glimpse of her today. She was so beautiful.
Maybe, even more beautiful than I'd ever realized.
It wasn't because of the way she was dressed.
It wasn't because of the way her hair was styled, or the
color of it…nor its texture.
It wasn't because of her eye color, or of her skin.
And, it wasn't because of her shape.
As a matter of fact, her outer appearance had nothing to
do with the beauty before my eyes…because the
beauty that I saw, comes from within.

Her intellect and wisdom are her most appealing
qualities, allowing others to see her charm and
determination.
Her personality, partnered with her positive attitude,
makes her beauty impossible to ignore.
Strong is her will. Kind is her heart.
Disappointment has visited her, and brought with it
stress.
Heartache has stalked her, yet she's maintained the
courage to fight all negativity with the belief that she
is special and deserving of love and respect.
Her independence makes her admired, yet often
intimidating.
Her loyalty is the magnet that attracts true friends.
Her dependability is the glue that holds friendships
together.
Her confidence allows her to look in the mirror and
smile at herself.
Her ancestors hardships paved the way for her sense of
endurance and faith.
To appreciate her is desired.
To understand her is not always easy.

To love her is expected.

Who is this beautiful creature that I was privileged to see, who is far more beautiful on the inside, than on the outside?

She is a grandmother, a mother, a wife, a daughter…SHE is the essence of womanhood.

So, the next time you are in her presence, appreciate the beauty within. It's much more important than that which is only skin deep.

CaSaundra W. Foreman-Harris

ABOUT THE COVER

The cover of this book was designed by Sherman Howard, Jr., of Waco, TX.

The concept of the cover is this:

*There are no facial features because these faces could be anyone. Once you put features on their faces, they take on an identity.

*The different hairstyles represent the differences in personalities.

*The black dresses represent mourning and death.

*The white flowers on the dresses represent a carnation, which is a symbol for having a mother who's deceased.

*The imperfection of the artwork represents the fact that everyone has some imperfection; no body is perfect.

Printed in the United States
1040100001B